American Nature Writing
2003
10TH ANNIVERSARY

Celebrating Emerging Women Nature Writers

Edited by John A. Murray

Fulcrum Publishing
Golden, Colorado

For Alianor True

The quotations on page 3 (epigraph) come from a symposium on nature writing edited by John A. Murray, which appeared in the fall 1992 issue of *Manoa: A Pacific Journal of International Writing* (University of Hawaii Press).

Library of Congress Cataloging-in-Publication Data

American nature writing 2003 / selected by John A. Murray.
    p. cm.
ISBN 1-55591-353-9
1. Nature—Literary collections. 2. American literature—21st century.
I. Murray, John A., 1954–
PS 2003
8SXX'.XX—dc21 200300XXXX

Printed in the United States of America
0 9 8 7 6 5 4 3 2 1

Editorial: Daniel Forrest-Bank, John Mulvihill
Design: Anne Clark
Cover painting: *Summer Storm,* oil on canvas, 16" x 20".
    Copyright © 2001 John A. Murray

Fulcrum Publishing
16100 Table Mountain Parkway, Suite 300
Golden, Colorado 80403
(800) 992-2908 • (303) 277-1623
www.fulcrum-books.com

American nature writing is energized by our most urgent social and political questions: how to live in right relationship. In learning to pay respectful attention to one another and plants and animals, we relearn the arts of empathy, and thus humility and compassion—ways of proceeding that grow more and more necessary as the world crowds in. I'm trying to say nature writing is in a period of great vitality because it is driven by a political agenda, as good art always is.

—William Kittredge

In my opinion, nature writing, including mine, is enjoying popularity in large part because Americans sense, and are worried about, their growing detachment from reality. ...[But] beset by a consumer society devouring itself, assaulted by flashing lights and screaming voices, breathing chemically treated air, and reading gibberish masquerading as wisdom, they haven't the energy or time for nature in the raw. By contrast, the nature writer can be seductive. ...Nature Herself doesn't bother with persuasion. In a world of change, nature is reliably unpredictable, and predictably more powerful than any human agency. Writers who learn from her can provide audiences with considerable hope and confidence, as we draw her lessons into poetry, politics, and, eventually, posterity.

—Linda M. Hasselstrom

Contents

Introduction by John A. Murray 6

1. EMMA BROWN 12
   Chamberlain (first publication)

2. VERNA JOHNSTON 19
   Redwood Forests
   (from *California Forests and Woodlands: A Natural History*)

3. CHRISTINE A. PETERSEN 37
   Shadows in Flight: Encounters with Bats
   (from *Bay Nature* magazine)

4. CHINLE MILLER 46
   Song of the Land (from *Plateau Journal*)

5. PENELOPE GRENOBLE O'MALLEY
   Urban Nature: Your Place or Mine (first publication) 61
   Are They More Moral in Montana? (first publication) 73

6. LEIGH CALVEZ 85
   A World Away (first publication)

7. LAURI DANE 96
   Where the Mountains Meet (first publication)

8. JENNIFER DEPRIMA 111
   Fire Line (first publication)

9. APRIL HEANEY 118
   The Garden of Live Flowers (first publication)

CONTENTS

10. GRETEL SCHUELLER 128
    At the Crossroads (first publication)

11. KIMBERLEY A. JURNEY 134
    Autumn 2001 (first publication)

12. DALE HERRING 141
    The Heron's Passport (first publication)

13. PENNY HARTER 145
    Poems (from *Buried in the Sky*)

14. ZORIKA PETIC 152
    Poems (from *Cascadilla Creek*)

15. ADELE NE JAME 160
    Poems (first publication)

16. JILL ROBIN SISSON 167
    Four Essays (first publication)

17. GRETCHEN DAWN YOST 186
    Hunting the Invisible (first publication)

18. JOHN A. MURRAY 203
    What We Found
    (from *Another Country: Encounters with the Red Rock Desert*)

Notes on Contributors 216
Permissions 220

Introduction

by John A. Murray

One touch of nature makes the whole world kin.
—Shakespeare

AMERICAN NATURE WRITING 2003 is the tenth volume in our series, and so, in a sense, it is the first anniversary volume. A tenth of a century has elapsed since its inception, and I am grateful to all—readers, writers, reviewers, editors, and publishers—who have faithfully supported the annual. Since the beginning, the series has been dedicated to featuring some of the best in contemporary nature writing, and this has included works of creative nonfiction, fiction, and lyric poetry. Sometimes nature has been at the margins of a particular piece. Other times it has been at the center. Always, the works have been touched and elevated in some significant way by that *other* world that surrounds and to no small degree sustains human civilization. From former President Carter to a convicted felon in an Arizona state prison, the writers have come from all walks of life and points of view, and have responded to nature in a fascinating variety of ways.

For the most part I have tried as an editor—and this has become increasingly so over time—to share with readers the writings of those who are at the beginning of their careers. It has often struck me that writers do some of their best—exciting and experimental—work in the early, ascent phase of their careers. Here can be detected the shape and substance of the good things that will emerge in the future. In Thoreau's younger years, for example, he produced such brilliant essays as "A Winter Walk," "Wild Apples," "Huckleberries," "Autumnal Tints," and "Natural History of Massachusetts." In these preliminary works we can detect the first stirrings of the master who would go on to compose "Walking" and *Walden*. The same is true of many other emerging nature writers who are living and breathing among us today. I feature them both because their work provides a glimpse into the future of American literature, and to nurture their careers, for nature will need all the help she can get in this challenging new century. Each of these writers will become a frontline advocate in what John Muir called "nature's green army."

To date, ten of the emerging writers featured in these pages—Sherry Simpson, Carolyn Kremers, Jennifer Brice, Marybeth Holleman, Louise Wagenknecht, Alianor True, Glen Vanstrum, Adele Ne Jame, Janisse Ray, Jan Grover—have gone on to publish books of their own. I congratulate them each on their achievement. Every book is a sacred artifact, the crystallization of a life, the confirmation of a calling, the sharing of a dream. The first four writers on the list all live in and write about Alaska. Sherry Simpson, whose essay "Where Bears Walk," was in the first collection, went on to publish *The Way Winter Comes* (Sasquatch), a collection of essays devoted to her experiences in the backcountry. Carolyn Kremers later published *Place of the Pretend People* (Alaska Northwest), a book that chronicled her life as a schoolteacher in the Yukon-Kuskokwim delta. Jennifer Brice wrote a book on interior life that was published by the University of Alaska Press, and Marybeth Holleman published a book of essays and photographs on Prince William Sound (Alaska Northwest).

The next three writers on the list reside in the American West. Louise Wagenknecht, whose writing I first encountered in the pages of *High Country News,* has gone on to write a memoir of growing up in the Pacific Northwest that will be published in 2003 by the University of Nebraska Press. Alianor True, who has worked as a seasonal firefighter in Grand Canyon National Park, Sequoia National Park, southern Nevada, and north-central Oregon, recently published *Wildfire* (Island Press), a comprehensive anthology of writings about fire management. Glen Vanstrum, who is a cardiac anesthesiologist in San Diego, has published a book of his essays with Oxford University Press (*The Saltwater Wilderness*). The book will explore his fascination—both as a scuba diver and underwater photographer—with the oceans of the world. Further to the west, Adele Ne Jame, an English professor at Hawaii Pacific University, has gone on to publish her first book of poems, *Field Work* (University of Hawaii Press).

The last two writers live and work east of the Mississippi. Janisse Ray, who lives on the edge of the Okefenokee Swamp, recently published *Ecology of a Cracker Childhood* (Milkweed Press), which received a favorable half-page review in the *New York Times Book Review* and was later the subject of a lengthy article in the same newspaper. Jan Grover wrote a compelling book, *North Enough: AIDS and Other Clear-cuts* (Graywolf Press) that explored the clear-cutting of the Upper Midwest forest as a metaphor for the destruction that AIDS visits upon the human body and spirit. Grover had previously worked for five years in San Francisco with patients afflicted with this disease.

Recently I sat down and read through all ten volumes in the series, this one included. As I read the approximately 200 selections I compiled a list of a few of my favorites. Many of the previous books, by the way, are still available through the publishers (1994, 1995, 1996, 1997, 1998, Sierra Club Books; 1999, 2000, 2001, Oregon State University Press; 2002, Fulcrum Books). Each reader will have his or her own list, of course, and all are valid, but here, for whatever it is worth, is mine (and in no particular order): Lisa Couturier, "Walking in the Woods" (1998); Emma Brown, "High Country" (2000); Alianor True, "Firefinder" (1998); Gretchen Dawn Yost, "Autumn in Love" (2002), John Haines, "Days in the Field" (1996); Annie Dillard, "On Bellingham Bay" (1994); Peter Matthiessen, "At the End of Tibet" (1995); Jimmy Carter, "The Forty-Ninth State, But Not in Fishing" (1996); E. O. Wilson, "Biodiversity Threatened" (1995); Edward Abbey, "Sheep Count" (1994).

Beginning last year, I instituted the William O. Douglas Nature Writing Award. It carries with it no wooden plaque or gilded trophy, no sheepskin certificate, no monetary compensation—for the authentic writer does not write for payment but rather from the happiness that derives from pursuing truth and beauty. The award carries with it only the knowledge that this editor, for whatever it is worth, found a particular work to be the best that crossed his desk in the previous year (not the "best" of that year, but the "best to cross his desk"—there is a difference). It is named in honor of one of the seminal figures in the environmental movement. William O. Douglas served on the Supreme Court from 1939 to 1975. During his tenure Douglas, among other things, authored *A Wilderness Bill of Rights* (1965) and wrote the 1972 court opinion stating that wilderness has a right to legal standing in the courts (*Sierra Club v. Morton*). Douglas was also an ardent environmentalist (helping to form what is now the Arctic National Wildlife Refuge) and a distinguished nature writer (*Farewell to Texas: A Vanishing Wilderness, My Wilderness: East to Katahdin, My Wilderness: The Pacific West*). The award is meant to set the literary bar as high as possible, to encourage writers to always tell the truth, to remind us of the importance of making a difference, and to honor good work well done.

This year's award goes to the writing of Emma Brown, whose work has been featured in two other volumes in the series (the essay "High Country" in *American Nature Writing 2000* and the essay "Climbing Fremont" in *American Nature Writing 2001*). At twenty-three, Emma Brown is one of the most gifted young writers I have ever encountered, and that includes the over six hundred undergraduate and graduate students I taught during my years as a university writing professor. Emma Brown grew up in Arlington, Virginia, the daughter of a professional newspaper journalist. After completing her degree in history at Stanford University, she moved to Juneau, Alaska. Her youthful travels have so far taken her to the Andes of Peru, the Baja peninsula, the Wind River Range of Wyoming, and the mountains of Idaho.

Many of the diverse themes and points of view present in the 2003 collection are evident in her essay, "Chamberlain," as she explores the place of humankind on the planet, the possibilities of achieving a communion with the landscape, and the nature of grace. At points the prose evokes the best of such diverse writers as Edward Abbey and Norman Maclean—an instinctive grasp of language and a quiet pilgrimage toward liberation and renewal.

The difference, of course, is that, at twenty-three, neither Abbey nor Maclean was writing as well as Emma Brown. If William O. Douglas could be reconstituted, he would feel completely comfortable in Emma Brown's world—the essays and the woods and worn keyboard of the loyal knight.

As always, I invite my readers to send me their work (P.O. Box 102345, Denver, Colorado 80250). I am especially interested in writing from underrepresented regions of the country (the Northeast, the Midwest, the Deep South), from those who write of nature in the urban or suburban context, from those known only locally or regionally (or perhaps not at all) but with national potential, and from those with writings inspired by travel abroad. The selections do not have to be strictly natural. I invite essays, stories, and poems in which nature is on the margins as well as those in which it is the focal point. Chiefly, I am attracted to writing that is original in voice and perspective and that evidences excellence in craft. The best way for a potential contributor to achieve a sense of my editorial approach is to review the selections in the ten volumes to date.

Thank you, dear friends, for having lovingly nurtured this series with your bookstore choices and kind submissions and welcome inquiries. Your warm and friendly cards, letters, and packages are truly cherished—I always open them first, and an unexpected salutation is always a wonderful way to start the morning. Working together, readers, writers, and editors, we can keep the *American Nature Writing* series alive and well in this challenging new century. This effort, we can be sure, will be as beneficial for literature and nature as it will be for the society that is sustained by literature and nature.

Chamberlain

Emma Brown

HALLIE AND I STEPPED OFF a Greyhound bus at a gas station in McCall, and from there some tiny plane whisked us to someplace we couldn't have imagined. It was a meadow, a green-soaked June meadow that spread out along a creek, and at its edge cabins hid in the lodgepoles. We unloaded our backpacks in the drizzle and a small woman named Margaret squished through mud in rubber boots, then welcomed us with delicate hugs. She said, you are here, this is home, Chamberlain Station.

There is no telling how a strong and inexact yearning translates into movement, into change, into watching raindrops gather into great raging creeks here in central Idaho. I hadn't known what to want. I saw an ad for a job with the Forest Service. I was eighteen years old and in school near San Francisco, where professors lectured inside dark halls while rush-hour traffic bore down. I couldn't listen, and instead looked out the window to foothills carpeted with stiff grass and live oaks, and beyond to the green coast range that hid the Pacific. I sat looking out at the alive world, and felt my whole life had been spent this way.

But there was that ad, and it promised superlatives: the largest wilderness in the Lower Forty-Eight, the largest herds of elk in the Rockies, strenuous work, solitude. The words conjured an imagination of daily exhaustion, simple thought, and open space. And that blurry vision seemed enough—I would find quiet, there would be plenty of time and mosquitoes, I would become strong. I applied, and the Forest Service took me.

Across the country on a Massachusetts island, a woman named Hallie was reading the same advertisement. She was lifeguarding at the local swimming pool, taking college courses, falling out of love, and mediating arguments between her father and her mother. Hallie applied, and the Forest Service took her.

In early June, Hallie said good-bye to her baby-blue truck and her feuding parents and to the man she didn't love anymore, and she traveled west; I finished final exams and packed my bags until late in the night and traveled east. We met in the Boise airport, exhausted and thrilled. We each had a backpack bulging with everything we would need for three months. It was not a lot to hold on to in the middle of so much unknown country.

And then, and suddenly, we were here, knowing now why we had come. Margaret because she had been coming for thirty years and this, truly, was home. Hallie and I because it was as far away from home as we could imagine, and it was wild. The country swallowed us up and hid us for three months while we exhausted ourselves at our job, at this outdoor living, while we rested from the world.

The Forest Service hired us to keep their trails in order, and so we did: we got good with the ax, and after a time we could make our crosscut sing through fallen trees. At night, miles from Chamberlain, we'd eat too little and then crawl into sleeping bags

13

mosquitoes whine against the screen. No one used our
that we saw; hunters would arrive in October for elk
id the first snows, but now during summer the place was
pled. We were grateful.

In early summer before we knew each other well, Hallie and I
ft our cabin for just the day in search of trees and puddles in the
way of our trail. We lunched on peanuts and sandwiches, then
came to a creek that crossed the trail. Hallie went first with her
boots slung over her neck; the water crawled over her knees to her
thighs as she howled from the cold. She retreated, uttered a low
whistle, and said the water was deep. We undressed then, and
though it was sunny and June, the wind raised goose bumps on
our skin. I started across and lost my breath when the water crept
up to my crotch. The snowmelt rushing down from the ridges
above swelled around our ribs, urging us to follow it downstream;
the cold rush of it made Hallie hoot and whoop behind me while
I whispered o my god.

On the other side, we breathed hard, we groaned, and we
danced to make ourselves warm. I dried myself with a shirt while
Hallie studied the map and decided there was no need for shoes,
or even clothes. She was grinning. We'd cross this creek again in
a quarter mile. We shouldered our backpacks, our ax and shovel
and six-foot crosscut saw, and we tromped down the trail, side by
side, breeze tickling our stomachs and pebbles catching between
our toes.

I turned around, looking back for whatever we might have left
behind, and saw endless pairs of eyes strung out among the trees.
I poked Hallie and we watched together. Elk stared back with
wide eyes, until some movement caused them to turn together
and bolt. The herd ran, and the earth trembled; the vibrations

came up through our feet into our chests, and we stood and watched them go. The thunder receded and Hallie burst into laughter. I saw her in profile, and the sun shone through her teeth when she tossed her head back. Look at us! she cried. They were stunned by us! And we stepped back and looked at ourselves, brown triangles of pubic hair still dripping with creek water and our tools slung over our shoulders, mud climbing up our legs. Hallie beamed, struck silly by being caught in our nakedness by a herd of surprised elk, and I laughed out loud. We turned, and headed down our trail, breathless. The sun warmed our bottoms as we went.

Later, thunderheads grew until they collapsed into rain. Our shorts clung to our legs and our jackets hung heavy under the weight of water by the time we recrossed the creek on our way home. We were hurrying back to our one-room cabin and its wood-burning stove; we didn't bother with undressing. The elk were absent this time, but the mud on the bank of the creek remembered them with hundreds of hoofprints that now acted as miniature cisterns, collecting the rain.

On the other side I hung back and watched Hallie's dark braid weave in and out of trees. I sang as I walked; the sound was dampened by raindrops and wet ground. At the cabin, we pinned our wet clothes to a line over the stove and we boiled water for hot chocolate. Hallie was lighting a lamp when she flashed her eyes at me and said, That was a good day. I agreed, and then the lamp was lit and we sat to watch the rain wet our meadow in gray sheets.

Fires are usually named after identifying geographical features. In spring, Flossie Creek had rushed behind the cabin Hallie and I shared; in summer it had been not much more than a trickle. Flossie Lake lay six miles away up winding switchbacks. The Flossie Fire sat quietly among a litany of wildfires in last August's National Fire Situation Report. I called the Payette National Forest; a woman there told me that the fire had long since burned over Chamberlain Station. The buildings were saved, she said, but nothing else. The fire is forty thousand acres and growing, she continued. It's windy, she said. It's dry. These fires'll go out when the snow flies.

And I was glad, mostly, that the thick forests surrounding Chamberlain were left alone to burn, as is their way. But I cried, too, for the loss of my place there.

People say it is best to live in the present. Buddhists say it; yoga instructors say it; mystics say it; therapists say it. I have tried to follow their advice, but am daily and inevitably swept into memory. I have held on tightly to the corner of earth between Chamberlain Creek and the Salmon River. Not because it was perfect, or because it was not perfect—but because I can't bear to leave it behind. That cabin on the edge of the meadow, and the trails that radiated out in all directions, and the streams that crossed the trails on their journey to the sea—I was born in these places. I memorized that country's fallen trees and puddled trails at the same time that I was unearthing myself, growing into a brown angled body and a new rhythm of active meditation. I can't remember what that feels like, that sort of tempestuous personal change, and so I have placeholders—concrete details that can trigger Then's intangibles. I have one morning when the trees on the east side of the meadow were blackened by the backlight of a rising sun, and I have the taste of ripe huckleberries in late August, when the grasses had settled into brown. I carry these artifacts of myself—I refer to them when I begin to forget who I have been.

I thought these snapshots would tide me over until I returned, and then everything would be displayed with the kind of richness the mind does not provide. It turns out, however, that memorized details will have to suffice. My place is changed; now the naked tops of black trees pierce the sky; the smell of old smoke has overtaken that of tarweed and lupine. Trails are thick with trees whose roots, burnt through, weren't enough to hold them during winter storms. The herds of elk are smaller; some died in the fires, and others died when snow came and the fires had taken their winter forage. This spring the earth will rebound; fire-death gives new life to a forest, and I am glad for that. But it's one thing to know that life renews itself on a grand scale after this burning, and quite another to feel on a smaller, more personal scale the loss of a beloved place.

I don't know where Hallie is anymore, but I meet people who have known her. She built trails in Alaska and she was in love with a boy who traveled with her across America, and someone said she was finishing college. I think of her; I even write her, but the letters get lost under beds and stacks of paper, or they are folded in a pocket and then ruined in the wash before they are paired with an envelope. Sometime we'll see one another, if just for an afternoon; I'm not sure whether we'll have much to say about how our lives have been since then, about our lives back in the world of cars and family, lovers and bright lights. We will say, do you remember?

And then conversation will tumble into memory and wonder: the goodness of Margaret's homemade skillet bread after days of hunger and labor, our arrival at the Salmon River after a long day of treading through wildflowers, and the meadow outside our cabin that over the course of the summer dried from soaking green to golden and, just before we left, brown. We might try to speak out loud the shock of snowmelt-swollen creeks around our midriffs, the freedom of our own naked bodies, and the hilarity of sharing place, discovery, and ourselves with a herd of wide-eyed elk. And then we might decide not to speak of it at all; we might realize that delight is best remembered by laughter, easy company, and simple knowledge that we are tied by what we have shared.

Redwood Forests

Verna Johnston

MAJESTICALLY TALL, IMPRESSIVELY OLD, the Redwood (Sequoia sempervirens) forms forests of world-renowned beauty along the rainy Pacific Coast of northern and central California. From just south of Big Sur to slightly beyond the Oregon border, its tall spires dominate the lowlands and lower mountain slopes of the Coast Ranges in a roughly 10-mile-wide belt. Never continuous, the forests are intermittent in the south and relatively unbroken only from central Humboldt County north.

The largest, most magnificent groves thrive in the northwestern corner of California, many of them in state and national parks. Here the trees reach maximum heights in lush rain forest surroundings. Growing arrow-straight, their elegant reddish brown boles rise 200 to 300 feet high (90 m) from a forest floor often hidden by mosses, ferns, and herbs. Climbing up through the traceries of taller shrubs to form a green canopy far above, many individuals surpass 300 feet (90 m). A tree in Redwood National Park, known simply as Tallest Tree, holds the world's record at 368 feet (111 m). Its 10-foot (3 m) diameter is not unusual. Ten to 15-foot breadths (4.5 m) are common.

While Redwood trees are the tallest in the world and grow to venerable ages (1,000 to 2,220) years, they are not nearly as big around as their Sierra Nevada cousin, Giant Sequoia *(Sequoiadendron giganteum),* nor as old as the Western Bristlecone Pine *(Pinus longaeva)* of California's White Mountains. But Redwoods' old-growth forests emanate very special moods unique to them. Somber and hushed in the fogs, cathedral-like when the sun radiates through canopy openings, they generate a serenity that slows the pace and takes you back in time.

Redwood family lineage does go back geologically to the Age of Dinosaurs. Fossils indicate that one hundred million years ago Redwoods of a dozen species spread widely over western North America, Europe, and Asia in a climate much milder than today's. Ice ages, volcanic eruptions, uplifts of mountain ranges, continental drift, and drastic climate changes all took their toll on population survival over the millennia.

By the end of the Ice Ages the Redwood species in North America had shrunk to two. The range of the two survivors dwindled to a fraction of its former size. Giant Sequoia continued to flourish only in isolated groves of California's Sierra Nevada. The Redwood, often called Coast Redwood, was restricted to its narrow coastal belt. Today, by common usage, the name "Redwood" refers to the California coastal species alone.

Redwood Forests thrive in a mild maritime climate with heavy winter rains up to 100 inches (250 cm), frequent storms, and cool summers with dense night and morning fogs. Averse to salt spray, the trees generally live inland from the ocean just far enough to avoid it. Mendocino County has some exceptions. Following the wide river valleys as far as the ocean fogs penetrate, Redwood stands often occur up to 30 miles (50 km) from the coast in the north.

Wherever they grow, their massive crowns comb huge quantities of moisture from the mist and let it fall as "fog drip" to the forest floor, adding the equivalent of 12 inches (30 cm) or more of precipitation during the rainless summer months. Abundant water, high humidity, and the dense shade cast by the tall trees are the prime environmental ingredients with which Redwood Forests "create their own localized climate" (Becking 1982: 1).

The trees themselves contribute heavily to the thick, life-sustaining litter of the forest floor. The litter's reddish brown hue comes largely from the branchlets of Redwood needles which fall to the ground in intact flat sprays when three or four years old. Mixed with these are the small, light brown cones, ¾ of an inch long (2 cm), that mature in October and November of each year. The trees are prolific cone bearers, but the seeds that fall out through cracks in the cone scales usually show a very low germination rate. Seedling establishment may be poor unless floods or fires create the special conditions that improve seedlings' chances.

Such disturbances have occurred periodically over the centuries. Within recent decades severe floods hit Humboldt County in 1955, 1964, 1974, and 1986. The floods of 1955 and 1964 provided a vivid picture of what happens to Redwoods along river bottoms in northern California in extreme high water. Edward Stone and Richard Vasey documented the results.

The December 1955 and January 1956 floods swept sawmills, farms, and whole communities down the Eel, Klamath, and Van Duzen rivers, disrupting transportation and communication, burying buildings under thick mud. The old-growth groves that dominated the alluvial flats (terraces of soil) deposited by floods along the Eel River were greatly reduced in size.

21

"Trees were uprooted and carried downstream, and the herbaceous cover within the groves was buried under 4 feet (120 cm) of stream-carried silt." Bull Creek, a tributary of the Eel, "turned into a raging torrent, uprooted more than 300 (mature) Redwoods" and washed away some of the flats on which they had grown (Stone and Vasey 1968: 157). Weakened stream banks caused later loss of 224 more large trees to erosion.

When Paul Zinke studied an exposed stream bank face along Bull Creek, using radiocarbon dating, he found that this sort of devastation was not new. "Fifteen major floods in the past 1,000 years have caused the deposition of sufficient silt (each forming a distinct profile) to raise the elevation of these alluvial flats more than 9 m [30 feet]" (Stone and Vasey 1968: 158). Periodic erosion, followed by flooding and silt deposits on river flats downstream, has apparently been part of a natural Redwood environmental pattern for thousands of years.

Redwoods are well equipped to handle such disastrous environmental changes. When their trunks are buried beneath flood-carried silt, the trees sprout new roots that grow vertically upward from the buried ones, sometimes so strongly that the root tips come shooting through the surface. Later, a new more permanent horizontal root system spreads out from the trunk below ground and replaces the short-term vertical one. Since Redwoods may be buried many times in their long life of 600 to 2,000 years or so, they develop a multistoried root system, a new set for each flood they survive.

Redwood trees have a tap root, but it is their shallow roots, stretching wide and interweaving with those of neighboring trees, that give them a firm base. This adventitious system works well, but, in some areas, makes the trees vulnerable to windthrow unless flooding and siltation provide soil for new roots and added support.

The roots are sensitive, however, to compaction of the soil and may be suffocated by gravel and logging debris that does not allow soil aeration. Road building, clear-cutting, and skidding of logs in the past 100 years have drastically altered the natural pattern of flooding. Roads interfere with natural runoff on hillsides, causing landslides and heavy soil erosion. Clear-cutting, the removal of all, or nearly all, trees, adds to both erosion and landslides and makes the remaining trees more subject to windstorm damage. All of these increase the sediment in streams below.

When there is more sediment entering a river than the river can carry away, the excess piles up on flats and sandbanks in midstream. The main current is forced toward the bank, undercutting trees growing there. More than 100 old-growth Redwoods along the Avenue of the Giants, and ten in the Richardson Grove, were undercut and killed this way in the flood of 1986, when 23 inches (57 cm) of rain fell in 9 days along the South Fork of the Eel River.

The silt left by floods creates new Redwood habitat at the expense of that which is washed away. Siltation gives the trees the chance to grow more adventitious roots, which provide the support needed to grow taller, bigger, and older. And siltation provides the mineral seedbed needed by seedlings.

In addition to floods, Redwoods have been exposed to fire over the centuries. And, here too, they are superbly adapted to survive. Their tough, fibrous bark, 6 to 12 inches thick (30 cm), does not burn easily. The large amount of water in their wood and their almost nonflammable pitch resist fire. But if a fire is severe enough, it will eat its way through the protective bark and open up the underlying wood to the next fire that comes along, eventually giving flames access to the heart of the tree. Most Redwood groves show some trunks with fire-blackened cavities.

Fire and flood both create the disturbances on the forest floor that encourage next spring's Redwood seedlings to get started. The exposed mineral soil, free from root-attacking fungi previously in the litter, gives them a better chance to survive if they are in enough sunlight to photosynthesize (produce food) and in enough soil moisture to keep their roots alive.

Redwood seedlings often become established on decaying down logs and upturned roots. Many die as the "punky" wood dries. Once established, however, even in extreme shade, a Redwood may survive in a suppressed condition for hundreds of years until an opening in the canopy permits it to shoot on up. Emanuel Fritz watched this happen to a 160-year-old Redwood that stood 100 feet tall in the understory beneath 300-foot-high giants. Once released by an opening far above, this tree, which had been growing at less than one percent a year, suddenly grew at 20 percent a year for the next 10 years.

Disturbances of any kind also bring out one of the Redwood's most remarkable traits, virtually unknown in conifers—its ability to sprout new stems and roots from burned, cut, or blown-down trunks. From the time that it is very young, a Redwood seedling carries latent buds around its base and along its trunk. When damaged or irritated, these dormant buds develop into leafy shoots and roots and, eventually, whole new trees. Masses of dormant buds, known as burls, bulge out like tumors on the trunks of some trees. Much sought after for their gnarled, twisted grains, burls produce beautiful designs and color effects when smoothed and polished.

The "fairy rings" of Redwood trees in many groves are the end result of prolific sprouting. An original monarch, badly burned, sprouts a dozen or more shoots all around its base. Three or four of these survive and grow into mature trees, circling the parent tree, which eventually dies. The survivors, in turn, if injured, produce sprouts around themselves, some of which survive. Over the centuries a ring of trees may stand around long-gone ancestors. This sprouting ability explains why there are still Redwoods growing on logged-over forests that have failed to regenerate new seedlings.

The natural floods and fires that have swept through the coastal forests over time have not only made seedling establishment possible but have actually helped the Redwoods maintain dominance over their competitors. Douglas-Fir *(Pseudotsuga menziesii)*, Tan Oak *(Lithocarpus densiflorus)*, Grand Fir *(Abies grandis)*, and California Bay *(Umbellularia californica)*, living on the surrounding slopes, all drop their seeds onto the same river-edge soils as the Redwood does. But all these are easily killed by fire, as they lack the protection of Redwood's thick bark.

The Tan Oaks of the Redwood Forest understory sprout vigorously after fires. They also tolerate shade and share with the Redwood a first-class defense against insects, fungi, and rot, namely wood and bark impregnated with tannin. But Tan Oak, along with Douglas-Fir, Grand Fir, and California Bay, succumbs to flooding and silting. Redwood survives both. Hence, on the river benches and floodplains of northern California, Redwood dominates the lowland areas. The tallest, oldest, most venerable Redwoods grow here.

⌒

But on the upland slopes, which are extensive, Redwood intermingles with the other conifers and hardwoods in forests that take on a true canopied look. Old-growth Redwoods and Douglas-Fir form the tall upper tier of the canopy. Douglas-Fir often dominates on shallow soils of steep slopes. Beneath their crowns grows an understory of Tan Oak, Pacific Madrone *(Arbutus menziesii)*, and companion hardwoods. Below that tier a layer of shrubs and ferns proliferates—huckleberries, Western Sword Fern *(Polysticum munitum)*, shrubby Tan Oak. Under these, on the forest floor, a ground cover of herbs flourishes—Redwood Sorrel *(Oxalis oregana)*, Vanilla Leaf *(Achlys triphylla)*, False Lily-of-the-Valley *(Maianthemum dilatatum)*, and others.

Douglas-Fir is the most common associate of Redwood in the tall, upland forests—a handsome tree with slightly weeping branches and soft, blunt needles. Its fallen cones, with the identifying three-pronged bracts protruding between the scales like whiskers, give away its presence. Douglas-Fir accompanies Redwoods through their entire north-south range and becomes a major component of the drier forests to the east of the Redwood belt, as well as of the rain forests in Oregon and Washington.

The Grand Fir, an equally imposing tree, frequently grows to 180 feet high (54 m), with long branches and 1 to 2-inch needles (5 cm) that are a deep shiny green above and carry two bands of whitish stomata (breathing pores) on the lower surface. Grand Firs mix with Redwoods intermittently near the coast from Mendocino County northward but drop out a few miles inland.

The most abundant broad-leaved evergreen of the upland forests, Tan Oak, also known as Tanbark Oak, produces acorns like oaks but flowers and leathery leaves that resemble those of chestnuts and chinquapins. Indeed, the species is considered a possible connecting link between oaks and chestnuts. More than one hundred of Tan Oak's nearest relatives grow natively in

Indomalaysia and Southeast Asia. Its bark once provided the chief commercial Western source of tannin. Its acorns still furnish food for Black Bears *(Ursus americanus)* and Black-tailed Deer *(Odocoileus hemionus columbianus)*.

Yellow-rumped Warblers *(Dendroica coronata)*, and other small birds, enjoy the black berries of another common understory tree, Wax Myrtle *(Myrica californica)*. Nomadic Band-tailed Pigeons *(Columba fasciata)* sometimes swoop down to gorge on the orange-red berry crop of the reddish-barked madrones. Madrones, curving up to find scarce light among the taller trees, add white jug-shaped flowers in summer and large glossy leaves the year around to the forest scene. Tolerating moderate shade, they sprout readily from the stump after burning.

Another stump sprouter, Giant Chinquapin *(Chrysolepis chrysophylla)*, occasionally becomes a fairly large tree in the understory of Redwood Forests. One of only two North American representatives from a primarily tropical Asian group, it bears narrow, leathery evergreen leaves up to 4 inches long (10 cm) which are dark green above and golden hairy below. Its distinctive burry fruit holds a sweet, purplish seed that is very popular with chipmunks.

Relatively uncommon needle-bearing trees that lack the seed cones of full-fledged conifers but grow among them include Pacific Yew *(Taxus brevifolia)* and California Nutmeg *(Torreya californica)*. Yews form a part of the shady understory. Slender trees with thin bark that flakes off in rosy purple scales and downward sweeping branches of unequal length, they often present a somewhat scraggly profile. Their flat, two-ranked shiny green needles come to a point and slightly resemble those of Redwood. However, yew needles are pale green underneath, whereas Redwood's are whitish. In autumn the female trees produce seeds in juicy scarlet cups (arils) on the undersides of leafy twigs. The fruits appeal to many birds who eat the edible red flesh and scatter the poisonous seeds. The bark of yew yields Taxol, an important anti-cancer drug.

The attractive, dark green California Nutmeg grows singly or in scattered small stands, easily recognizable by the sharp, stiff prickle at the tip of each 1½-inch needle (4 cm). The crushed needles give off a peculiar odor, hence the name "stinking yew." The fleshy "fruit," borne on the separate female tree, looks a little like the commercial nutmeg of the tropics, though unrelated. It resembles a greenish plum with a large seed.

In Russian Gulch State Park on the Mendocino Coast, California Nutmeg attains possibly its largest size. A record tree near Fort Bragg stood 141 feet high (42 m) with a girth of over 14 feet (4 m) until cut by timber vandals in the early 1980s. Most nutmegs are much smaller. They stump sprout and grow almost as rapidly as Redwoods when young. It takes a special hunt to find them.

The search for an albino Redwood is much more difficult. These forest phantoms have been known since the 1860s, written about by Willis Linn Jepson and by Emanuel Fritz. Fritz, one of the world's authorities on Redwoods, called "Mr. Redwood," said that he had seen perhaps ten in his long life. Loggers, botanists, and others who have found them usually form an unofficial protection society by not revealing their sites.

The rare white Redwood is a true albino: its leaves and stems are totally white. Lacking the genes for chlorophyll synthesis, it survives by tapping the root system of its parent. It is usually one of many sprouts from a parent stump's "sucker patch." The largest one recorded stood 80 feet high (24 cm) compared to the towering 200 to 300 feet (90 m) of green Redwoods. Most white

Redwoods are much smaller, modest shrublike growths under 5 feet tall, through 20 to 30-foot individuals have been discovered. At any height, the unique albino is an unusual phenomenon in a Redwood Forest.

Redwood prefers sedimentary soil and will not usually invade other types. Where certain nonsedimentary soils intrude into a Redwood area, Coastal Prairies appear. In one such open grassy area in Prairie Creek Redwoods State Park, Roosevelt Elk *(Cervus elaphus roosevelti)* commonly graze.

Weighing well over 500 pounds, with massive antlers, the bulls are an impressive sight. During the fall rutting season, spectacular battles occur as the dominant bull clashes with rival males who challenge his possession of the harem. Once more widely ranging throughout northwestern California, elk now form fewer herds here. In coastal Oregon and Washington they still roam freely through dense forests and brush fields interspersed with meadows.

The greatest diversity of plant and animal life in the Redwood region occurs along the rivers and creeks flowing out to sea through breaks in the Coast Ranges. Here the sun penetrates along natural edges, and in the nesting and flowering months of May and June a whole riparian community bursts into life. Big-Leaf Maple *(Acer macrophyllum)* and gray-barked Red Alder *(Alnus rubra)* share the creekside habitat with berry thickets. Bogs mingle the spathes of Yellow Skunk Cabbage *(Lysichiton americanum)* with the veiled green of Giant Horsetails *(Equisetum telmateia)*. Sometimes the horsetails reveal a yellow-green, 4-inch-long Banana Slug *(Ariolimax columbianus)* wrapped around a jointed stem, sleeping, breathing through a hole in its side, its eyes black dots on the ends of larger tentacles.

Wilson's Warblers *(Wilsonia pusilla)* chant from the willows (Salix spp.). Dippers *(Cinclus mexicanus)* fly low over the water and disappear beneath the surface in their search for caddisfly and mayfly larvae. A Belted Kingfisher's *(Ceryle alcyon)* rattle downstream signals its hunt for unwary salmon or steelhead fingerlings.

The Winter Wrens *(Troglodytes troglogdytes)* that were singing breathless songs from shaded stumps in late April are now busy feeding their fledglings. These demanding balls of dark brown feathers buzz and trill in and out of log tangles, landing on fern fronds that hardly ripple under their weight.

From an alder, Swainson's Thrush *(Catharus ustulatus)* notes spiral up the scale. Where the trail crosses the creek, half a dozen Chestnut-backed Chickadees *(Parus rufescens)* all bathe at one time in little puddles, descending from hillside Douglas-Firs and Tan Oaks with buzzy "dee-dee-dees" to splash in the watery depressions. An American Robin *(Turdus migratorius)* digs between creek pebbles, one eye on a chipmunk darting nervously in for a quick drink. And from up among the dark trees the haunting atonal notes of the Varied Thrush *(Ixoreus naevius)* echo through the forest.

In June the Red Elderberries (Sambucus racemosa) along the creek hang heavy with their annual crop of berries. The flat-topped white flower heads and huge leaves of Cow Parsnip *(Heracleum lanatum)* stand waist high alongside bushes of Cascara *(Rhamnus purshiana)* and Western Azalea *(Rhododendron occidentale)*. Song Sparrows (Melospiza melodia) in the Thimbleberry *(Rubus parviflorus)* and California Blackberry *(Rubus ursinus)* bushes seem to be endlessly tuning up.

Along the creek banks and up the slopes, Man-root or wild cucumber (Marah spp.) twines among the shrubs, hiding well its emergence from a tuber as large as a man's body. Delicate saxifrages rim the wet spots. Red Columbines (Aquilegia spp.) mingle with clumps of Lady Ferns *(Athyrium filix-femina)*, some ferns just unfurling the frond tip, others with crescent-shaped sori already developing on the under side. The Five Finger Ferns *(Adiantum aleuticum)* carry anywhere up to sixteen "fingers."

The creeks and streams in the Redwood belt are themselves home to Silver Salmon *(Onchorhynchus kisutch)* and Steelhead Trout *(Onchorhynchus mykiss)* which cast shifting shadows on the gravelly sand and gray-bouldered bottom. During the rains of December, January, and February, the fish make their way from the ocean upstream to spawn. The adult salmon die after producing eggs and milt, but their young hatch in early spring and remain in the pools until next winter's rains raise the creek levels high enough for them to swim to sea. There they grow to mature size and in two years return to the streams in which they were born to continue the cycle.

Steelhead, ocean-going trout, do not die after spawning and may make three or four spawning runs in their lifetime. Their fingerlings spend one or two years in the creeks before heading out to sea.

These same creeks serve as important breeding arenas for many of the abundant amphibians in the Redwood belt. Pacific Giant Salamanders *(Dicamptodon ensatus)*, Red-bellied Newts *(Taricha rivularis)*, Tailed Frogs *(Ascaphus truei)* and others lay eggs in the cold waters, and their larvae grow to adulthood there.

Still other salamanders, as well as reptiles like the Rubber Boa *(Charina bottae)*, the Ringneck Snake *(Diadophus punctatus)*, which turns orange belly up when disturbed, and the Sharp-tailed

31

Snake *(Contia tenuis)* which feeds entirely on slugs, live in rotting logs, beneath the bark of fallen trees, or burrow into the ground for the dry summer.

As with every ecosystem, a succession of flowers unfolds through the forest blooming season. The lovely Fairy Slipper or Calypso *(Calypso bulbosa)* ranks among the earliest. From February through May, its lone green basal leaf and short stalk topped by a delicate rose-pink orchid cover mossy logs in colonies or grow singly amid humus. It prefers the combined duff of Redwoods and Douglas-Fir but can survive in many mixed shade situations. And so low-growing is it that only a "belly view" will reveal its softly hairy throat and spotted lower lip.

The peak flowering period in the shaded Redwood Forests arrives in May. As the resident sword ferns shoot up fuzzy new fiddleheads, California Huckleberry shrubs *(Vaccinium ovatum)* produce pink and white flower bells beneath their shiny, saw-toothed leaves. Fragile-looking Sugar Scoop or Lace Flower *(Tiarella trifoliata)* covers acres with tiny white blossoms. Pink and white Star Flowers *(Trientalis latifolia)* rise on thin stalks above whorls of 3 to 6-parted leaves. Fairy Bells *(Disporum smithii)* hide creamy flowers under terminal parallel-veined leaves. Salal *(Gaultheria shallon)* overruns tangles with its thick, evergreen foliage and rows of white urn-shaped flowers, and the California Rose-Bay's showy rose clusters brighten many a trail *(Rhododendron macrophyllum)*.

Carpets of Redwood Sorrel spread heart-shaped leaflets everywhere over the spongy brown earth, leaflets so well adapted to the changing light and shade of the Redwood Forest that they droop dramatically in full sun, wilting from excessive water loss (transpiration). This very action reduces transpiration, allowing the leaves' vacuoles and intercellular spaces to fill up with water and expand again when back in the shade. When buried by silt, Redwood Sorrel grows vertical shoots to the new ground level, just as Redwoods do, and gradually recolonizes the forest floor. The plant is an indicator species of Redwood Forest.

The flowers of the forest floor could hardly be more distinct in size from the giants under which they grow. Yet, as Jepson has said, "the two, as living formations, belong together." The fossil record shows that they have come down through the ages, since before the Pleistocene epoch, linked for survival—the delicate flowers and the great red columns that provide their humus and shade (Jepson 1934: 12).

Tiny ants share the link as well. Many of the understory herbs, such as Bleeding Heart *(Dicentra formosa)* and Western Trillium *(Trillium ovatum)*, form seeds equipped with oil-bearing attachments that resemble dead insect parts. These attract scavenger ants, which carry off the seeds, feed on the oil attachments, and discard the seeds, dispersing the plants throughout the forest.

The shaded Redwood Forests house relatively few birds. An enormous quiet often settles among the trees, interrupted only occasionally by the croak of a Common Raven *(Corvus corax),* the tap of a woodpecker, the scold of a Winter Wren, the high, thin lisps of Golden-crowned Kinglets *(Regulus satrapa),* the harsh calls of Steller's Jays *(Cyanocitta stelleri).*

In recent years birders have added the loud, high "kree" notes of the Marbled Murrelet *(Brachyramphus marmoratus)* to the recognizable summer sounds of old-growth Redwood Forests.

The home life of this small, chunky seabird was an ornithological mystery for decades. Most other members of its family—puffins, guillemots, murres, auks, and auklets—nest in colonies on steep sea cliffs or offshore islands. All feed on ocean fish. But the Marbled Murrelet could never be found breeding near any of its relatives.

Then, in 1975, a Marbled Murrelet nest was discovered on a mossy limb 148 feet above the ground (44 m) in an old-growth stand of Douglas-Fir and Redwood in Santa Cruz County. The nest contained a single speckled green egg. It was in a tree 200 feet high (60 m), located about 6 miles inland from the nearest salt water. Research since then has pinpointed Marbled Murrelets' California nests primarily in closed canopy, old-growth Redwood Forests. The birds' calls are heard chiefly at sunrise and sunset as they fly over the tops of the trees or circle them before flying below the canopy. Resembling flying cigars with stubby wings beating rapidly, they vanish quickly into the tree crowns. In 1992, the California Department of Fish and Game listed the Marbled Murrelet as an endangered species in California. The bird's future within the state depends on survival of its old-growth forest habitat.

Most populations of birds and mammals of the Redwood Forests are found throughout the North Coastal Forests and Douglas-Fir/Mixed-Evergreen Forests of the region as well. Nocturnal mammals, such as Raccoons *(Procyon lotor)* and Striped Skunks *(Mephitis mephitis)* raid the campgrounds and hunt along the creeks. Bobcats *(Lynx rufus)* stalk Dusky-footed Wood Rats *(Neotoma fuscipes)*, chipmunks (Tamias spp.) and Brush Rabbits *(Sylvilagus bachmani)*. The Douglas Squirrels *(Tamiasciurus dou-glasii)* that scamper so acrobatically through the trees during the day, feeding chiefly on conifer seeds, sometimes fall victims to the pounce of Martens *(Martes americana)*. Actively hunting in early morning and late afternoon, these slender arboreal members of the weasel tribe, while rare, take their toll of Northern Flying Squirrels *(Glaucomys sabrinus)* discovered in tree holes, of birds and their eggs, and of any available prey.

Shrews (Sorex spp.) and Deer Mice *(Peromyscus maniculatus)* comb the forest litter. The high-strung shrews move about almost continuously, tracking insects, worms, and mice by scent. Shrews' tiny bodies, with a relatively large surface area and high metabolism, lose heat so rapidly that they must eat almost around the clock to stay warm and alive. Deer Mice, less frenetic feeders, consume a wide range of seeds, fruits, and insects.

In some of the shaded ravines inhabited by maples and alders, the unusual Shrew-Mole *(Neurotrichus gibbsii)* digs a network of runways deep in the forest litter. Mouse size, with the sensitive long nose of a shrew, it walks over the ground tapping it with the snout in its search for soil-dwelling pillbugs, centipedes, spiders, and insects. Its thick, heavy tail covered with stiff black hairs differs from the thin, mouselike tail of shrews.

All the interwoven plants and animals in the Redwood Forest ecosystem are tied intimately to the tall trees that shade them, the winter rains and summer fogs that water them, the mild maritime climate, the soil, the geography, and the accidents of history that brought them together in this singular natural home.

The Redwood's unique beauty, durability and usefulness as lumber has, however, proven to be its most vulnerable, almost fatal, feature. For during the last century, lumber companies have logged over 95 percent of the virgin Redwood Forests. Only about 2.5 percent remains in protected parks, and some of that, including the tallest trees of Redwood National Park, lies in lowland areas open to unprotected watersheds above.

Redwoods rank among the most resilient trees on earth. Adapted to naturally occurring floods and fires and able to resprout, they can turn a burned or cutover hillside into a green forest within a century. But during that century, the plants and animals dependent on the shade, soil moisture, shelter, and interrelated life of the old-growth ecosystem, will have died and vanished. And the second-growth forest replacement cannot begin to compare with the primeval beauty, the ambience, and the biodiversity of the 1,000-year-old forest gem long gone.

All of our remaining old-growth Redwoods, "standing tall" in their own special way among California's coniferous forests, deserve unequivocal protection from the bulldozer and the saw. We owe this one-of-a-kind Redwood Forest, and the future, no less.

Works Cited

Becking, Rudolf W. *Pocket Flora of the Redwood Forest.* Covelo, Calif.: Island Press, 1982.

Jepson, Willis A. *Trees, Shrubs, and Flowers of the Redwood Region.* San Francisco: Save the Redwoods League, 1934.

Stone, Edward C., and Richard B. Vasey. "Preservation of Coast Redwood on Alluvial Flats." *Science* 159 (3811): 157–161, 1968.

Shadows in Flight:
Encounters with Bats

Christine A. Petersen

TEN HOURS AGO, my hillside perch high above the fault-cut line of Northern California's Highway 1 offered a sweeping, sunlit view across Inverness Ridge and seaward into the heart of Point Reyes National Seashore. Five hours ago, as night closed in, the familiar forms of Firtop and Mount Wittenberg stood clearly silhouetted against a wash of stars and a waning crescent moon. Now, just after 3:00 A.M., even the most prominent coastal landmarks have faded behind a fine mist, which creeps in stealthily, dropping condensation that curls the edges of the papers on my clipboard. The night is chilly and damp, my only companions are a walkie-talkie and the occasional passing field mouse…and I couldn't be happier.

Despite the appearance (and sensation) of seclusion, I'm actually "keeping company" this night with several of the finest field biologists in the state. We're here as part of a multi-agency research project, using radio telemetry to observe the behavior of two of the park's most mysterious residents: Townsend's big-eared bats, and pallid bats.

Most folks would never guess it, but the nine counties encompassing the San Francisco Bay Area are a veritable haven for bats. To join the ranks of bat-watchers, make a sunset outing to your favorite outdoor haunt anytime between May and October. Visit Sunol Regional Wilderness, Tilden Park, or Foothills Open Space Preserve; stroll the landscaped campuses at Berkeley or Stanford. Take a seat on the beach at Bolinas, Pescadero, or Fort Funston. Occupy a bench beside one of the lakes in San Francisco's Golden Gate Park. As the light dims, focus your attention on the horizon, and scan the sky above the twilit crowns of trees. The movement around you will seem almost ghostly at first—just a flutter against the gloaming, a flash of streetlight glinting off sleek fur, a gentle ripple where wingtips, tiny feet, or mouth have just skimmed across the surface of a pond or stream. The shadows you see in flight, wherever you go, may be any of 14 bat species found in the Bay Area—from the ubiquitous little brown, big brown, or Mexican free-tailed bats, to diminutive western pipistrelles and sparrow-sized hoary bats.

If you prefer to keep your distance from bats, you're not alone. Still, take a moment to reflect on this remarkable group of mammals, which includes almost a thousand species worldwide and 24 in California alone. Singularly the top consumers of nocturnal insects, California's bats contribute substantially to the control of mosquito, fly, moth, and beetle populations. Nectar- and pollen-feeding bats play the same role as bees and hummingbirds by pollinating a wide variety of night-blooming plants, from crop fruits to tequila agave and saguaro cactus. And though we have none in the U.S., fruit-eating bats are seed dispersers essential to the health of rainforests. No human invention can replace these diverse ecological services, which bats have provided for at least 45 million years.

Over the past 150 years, as development has altered the California landscape, bats have faced the loss of roosting sites and the destruction of woodlands and waterways where they feed. Like birds, bats have been devastated by the use of pesticides that kill off their prey, contaminate water sources, and accumulate in their body tissues. Despite designation by the California Department of Fish and Game as Species of Special Concern, Townsend's big-eared and pallid bats—the species we're studying at Point Reyes and vicinity—are among the most threatened, victims of all these forces combined.

To make informed decisions about their protection into the future, our first job here is to clarify the bats' habitat needs—no small task, given that most species access three or more roosts over the course of a year, each roost with unique requirements. Winter hibernation sites must be free of disturbance and maintain a temperature at least a few degrees above freezing. Summer day roosts and maternity roosts, used for sleeping and raising pups, likewise should be fairly secluded, warm, and with a constant humidity. These are commonly found in caves, tree hollows or buildings, under rock crevices, tree bark or house shingles, or among clumps of leaves, depending on the species. While feeding, bats access night roosts within their foraging territory (barns, porches, and the undersides of bridges are common choices), where they can safely eat, digest, nap, and socialize between meals.

It is now late September. The bats' maternity season has concluded and the pups, born in May and June, are well on their way to independence, making it safe for us to undertake some hands-on research. Yesterday, biologists on the research team captured a dozen or so big-eared bats, and a handful of pallid bats emerging from their maternity roosts. Each was outfitted with the hippest of biological "jewelry": a shiny new one-gram radio transmitter, which was glued to each animal's shoulder fur (bats being too small to wear bulky radio collars). Thus placed, the tiny box and its antenna don't interfere with the bat's wing-beats, and aren't easily licked or bumped off. The transmitter's battery runs for about two weeks, roughly the same amount of time it takes for the glue to peel away.

Tonight, as on each of our ten allotted survey nights, research team members are dispersed far and wide around the park. Some of us remain, alone or in pairs, in one spot from dusk to dawn. Our job: find the bats by listening for their individual radio signals; document the location and direction of any movement; then pass the information along to mobile researchers, who dash from locale to locale trying to get close to each bat detected. Seemingly small details—whether the bat is stationary or in motion, in its day roost or holed up somewhere for a nighttime nap, feeding over water or some other habitat—are significant, because they reveal how the bats live out their night-to-night lives.

Like most of California's 24 species of chiropterofauna ("hand-wing animals"), pallid and big-eared bats were described and assigned scientific names in the mid-1800s. Beyond physical descriptions, however, the lives of bats remained mysterious until radio telemetry, night-vision scopes, and sophisticated acoustics gear were developed in the mid-1900s. Biologists now know far more about how particular bat species spend their time in and out of the roost. We're also discovering that social behavior, roosting and feeding habits, and seasonal activity patterns vary dramatically between bat species—and even within populations of the same species.

For example, while California's inland Townsend's big-eared bats commonly roost in caves and mines, coastal populations (having no access to caves) form maternity colonies in abandoned buildings and barns. When feeding, big-eared bats skim along the edges between forests and fields or over stream corridors, echolocating in search of small moths. Prey is grabbed in the claws or trapped in the membrane that stretches between the legs, then passed to the mouth and consumed mid-flight. Pallid bats take a different approach. While some choose buildings as day roosts, others opt for rock piles or crevices and hollows in oak trees. Pallids echolocate as a means of navigation, but not generally for feeding; instead they rely on their exceptionally acute hearing to detect the telltale movements of big, ground-dwelling insects—such as Jerusalem crickets, june bugs, and longhorn beetles—that are their prey. Prey is captured in the bat's sturdy jaws, then transported to a nearby night roost to be eaten.

Our current research objectives are to study how members of the Point Reyes population spend the few remaining days (and nights) of summer, and to learn when they disperse toward winter roosts. So here I sit in the damp darkness, awaiting signs of bats in motion. Every 15 minutes I stand up, adjust the strap of my radio telemetry receiver so that the weighty black box lies stable against my ribcage, and flip it on. I calibrate the frequency dial to 574, then—pointing the T-shaped hand-held antenna halfway between horizon and zenith—begin a slow clockwise circle starting at due north.

The female big-eared bat wearing transmitter 574 is nowhere to be heard. Resetting the dial to 529, I repeat the ritual, then again at 504. As I turn the antenna west, a series of loud pings suddenly peals out from the receiver. At the same time, a volley of rapidfire clicks erupts from my bat detector, proclaiming that 504 is flying close by. The detector is a clever little device that collects and records bats' echolocation calls, usually undetectable by human ears. As they fly, bats call out. By listening for echoes produced when those calls strike and are reflected by solid objects, a bat can tell how large an obstacle is, whether it is moving or stationary, and a plethora of other details that aid in navigation and isolation of even the tiniest flying insects. Though 504 sees respectably well (all "blind as a bat" myths aside), the big ears for which she was named—each about half her body length—are her real windows on the night-darkened world.

As I recite my coordinates into the walkie-talkie, a colleague announces, "504's east of the cemetery!" One of the mobile teams is nearby on Highway 1; they, too, are following the bat's movements. Over the next few minutes everyone listens with rapt attention, taking readings and scribing data as the bat flies slowly but deliberately southeastward, finally disappearing over the top of Bolinas Ridge...in the opposite direction from her usual day roost.

Throughout the next day we drive and hike the park's back roads, attempting to locate signals for the few bats who never returned to the day roost. One signal is located in a barn; a quick trip reveals that the transmitter has fallen off, probably while the bat was using the building as a night roost. A couple of other signals are impossible to locate; these bats may have moved beyond receiver range, perhaps towards winter hibernation roosts.

We're all especially fascinated by 504's retreat from the group roost—her signal pings steadily east of Bolinas Ridge, where there are no known colonies or even suitable buildings. Over the next few days, a concerted effort is made to discover where, exactly, she has holed up. Finally, the services of a local pilot and his twin-engine plane are called on, and the location of the signal is isolated from the air. Coordinates in hand, a bat biologist scrambles through the forest above Kent Lake and pinpoints the exact location of the bat's roost. Leaning inside the hollow of a tree, he points his flashlight upward. It reflects on the shiny metal of an almost-new radio transmitter antenna, and catches the coppery sheen of the fur on a snoozing Townsend's big-eared bat—the first ever found to roost in a tree. One mystery solved...and another handful of questions raised. Is this the bat's chosen place to sleep out the damp and mothless winter? If so, will other bats eventually join her here? Or is this just a way station en route to a more "permanent" winter roost? And might big-eared bats have used trees as day and maternity roosts in the era before buildings and mines became available, when old-growth trees were abundant? Sadly, with our limited time frame for research drawing to a close, further investigation of these questions must wait until another year.

Three weeks later, I'm seated cross-legged on the attic floor of a century-old redwood barn at the Laufenburg Ranch, near the Sonoma-Napa county line. The air is already thick with heat, though it's barely past nine o'clock on this October morning.

Thanks to the Sonoma Land Trust, which manages this lovely 175-acre spread, I've studied bats at Laufenburg Ranch over several consecutive summers. The ranch encompasses a mix of habitat types typical of the region, past and present: organic vegetable gardens and orchards leased by local farmers grow alongside native oak savanna, lush riparian woodland, and one of the most easterly redwood forests in the area. Consequently, it's home to a terrific sample of Bay Area bat species.

The barn is a real treasure, a testament to the ways in which bats have learned to live with humans. At any point in the spring, summer, or fall, I can enter this barn and find evidence of several species. Today, there's a hefty line of insect parts laid out directly below the attic's high central beam. It's unmistakably a pallid bat night roost, looking like a restaurant after the all-you-can-eat crab feast: beetle wing cases, antennae, and other inedible insect body parts are strewn hither and yon. The pallid bats' hard-shelled prey provides a bounty of meat, but requires work to access. Hanging in the night roost, they peel off the insects' hard exoskeletons, section by section, until the meat is accessible.

Climbing down from the attic, I give the barn's main floor a final shine-over with my flashlight in a cursory inspection for fresh guano (hard fecal pellets). A scattering of guano covers the seat of an old tractor in a storage room, where little brown bats like to sleep; dark oil stains below the tackroom's loose window frame show where Mexican free-tailed bats have been squeezing in. My last stop is an old horse stall at the building's darkest corner. Against the far wall, a few pieces of guano rest atop a stack of rickety wooden packing crates. To my surprise, the tiny pellets have a golden sheen. Only one bat I know of leaves such a distinctive calling card: the Townsend's big-eared bat, whose guano glitters with the undigested, iridescent scales of moth wings.

Not daring to move too fast, I drape my fingers over the flashlight to dim its glow, then point it upward. The small form is suspended by one foot from the ceiling just to my left, and she (or he) is awake. We watch each other for a few minutes, the bat's impressive two-inch ears—thin as paper—rotating and turning attentively to catch every nuance of sound in the dim room. Then, with a stretching rustle of her wings, this tiny living rarity settles in for a nap.

Though the weather retains its summery edge, the days are noticeably shorter and the nights are cool. Bats know the signs and respond accordingly. They're beginning to disperse, males and females seeking each other for their fall mating rituals, mothers and their young-of-the-year separating to fly in search of cozy winter haunts. Many of our local species undertake migrations, flying a few miles—or a few hundred miles—in search of suitable hibernation roosts or warmer winter feeding grounds. Yet the bat research community's knowledge of the big-eared bat's "ideal" hibernating site—a disturbance-free cave or mine that never freezes, located within 32 kilometers of the summer roost—gives me no way of knowing where this bat will sleep out the winter. The Bay Area has no suitable caves, and few hibernating big-eared bats have ever been found here. Perhaps it is for the best that some mysteries remain intact.

Moving slowly, I back out of the room, shut the half-door quietly behind me, and step out into the October sunshine. These last encounters will keep me bat-dreaming through the winter months, until warm summer nights draw the bats, and me, out into their world again.

Song of the Land

Chinle Miller

SUNRISE COMES BOLDLY, pushing wide orange blades of light over the horizon ahead of it, revealing austere gray hills where the now-retreating dark had settled for the night. As the dawn progresses, the monotone hills around me are transformed into various shades of yellow ricegrass, deep rich brown mudstone, and velvet-green stripes of Morrison Formation.

I stumble from my sleeping bag and start my ubiquitous morning coffee, or more appropriately, "black water," as the Zuni call it. To my south stretches Antelope Desert, that well-named flatland that separates Horseshoe Canyon and the San Rafael Reef. From the air, Antelope Desert looks like a long strip that keeps jagged cliff from falling into jagged canyon. Far to my north is Interstate 70 and Green River, Utah.

Coffee mug in hand, I begin to wander, intrigued by the microcosms of color everywhere, multi-colored rocks washed by bright sunlight. I pick up flakes of white pigeon-blood agate dotted with tiny drops of deep burgundy. I examine chunks of white agatized petrified wood laced with black manganese. Soon the light will lose its oblique angle and all this color will melt away in sun's unwavering heat.

The Sunday-afternoon artist in me wants to match each color with an oil palette, each with its own colorful name—cobalt blue, cadmium orange, rose madder. A piece of quartz catches my eye, laced with silvery veins that reflect the now-blue sky, creating a color I've never seen before—bluish-white-rose? I struggle with my need to label this unique tint until the light changes and it's gone, faded into a dull gray.

The strong coffee and warming air have awakened the linguist in me, and I begin wondering how my own native tongue, English, categorizes color. Blue, green, red, yellow—the base colors of the spectrum seem obvious, but why is there a term for that special shade of blue called cerulean and not one for the corresponding shade of green? I pick up a rock with tiny tiger-orange spots and wonder which colors are most common in nature.

Looking around me, I see an incredible array of not just primary colors, but of varying shades, hues, and intensities. How did the Native Americans of this region name these colors? Would their languages have the same categories as mine, would their words match my English lexicon?

Of course, the early natives of the Colorado Plateau didn't all speak the same language, at least so we hypothesize based on the disparity of their cultures. Many believe that the ancient ones who occupied the Four Corners region, the Ancestral Puebloans, were the ancestors of the modern Puebloans and thus spoke earlier versions of the Keresan and Tanoan language groups. Perhaps the Fremont, called "Moquis" ("dead ones") by the later Utes, left some yet-to-be-discovered clues to their language in the numerous rock panels that dot their homelands in the more northern sectors of the Colorado Plateau. Some speculate that the Fremont were early relatives of the Utes, although definitive archaeological evidence has yet to be found.

Much study has been made of Colorado Plateau rock art, with no linguistic significance found to date, although the possible symbolic nature of the numerous petroglyphs and pictographs has engaged many minds. The necessary precursor of written language is the development of symbols, but no evidence yet exists to indicate that the early Plateau dwellers, Puebloan or Fremont, had created a consistent system, although some believe that certain panels represent clan symbols, solar events, waterhole locations, and even maps.

But these early people are long-gone, and about all that's left, besides their rock carvings and the occasional potsherd and scraper, are the crumbled circular ruins of pithouses and the dreamy cliff-villages. And though some claim to hear the voices of the old ones whispering through the pinyon-juniper forests near the ancient ruins, the science of linguistics needs more than voices on the wind to decipher ancient languages.

Dawn has now melted into hot mid-morning, and as I make my way back toward camp, empty cup in hand, I notice a haze drifting in from the southwest, from the high Aquarius Plateau country. The color of the haze indicates a distant fire, and as it drifts in I watch the sky change from sky-blue to a shade of off-bluish-brown that I once again can't describe. I try to think of all the "blue" words in English—azure, indigo, royal, navy—but none of these work. English, that much-touted language of Shakespeare and the sciences, suddenly seems impoverished to me.

Perhaps I need a language closer to the landscape—or does such a thing exist? I think of my friend Antonio, a Ute Indian, who once told me, "Ute is an outdoor language. It helps you get along with the natural world, the real world."

Didn't we all once speak such outdoor languages, languages rich in terms for the natural world? As we have less occasion to use them, how many of these terms have changed meaning or simply passed from our vocabularies? And yet aren't we all ultimately still tied to our landscape? For many, this is now a landscape created by the human hand—the city, the urbanscape. Our language has coined new terms for this landscape ("smog," "gridlock"), even as the old terms pass out of usage ("copse," "bucolic").

But my landscape on this autumn day is the tableau of the Colorado Plateau, the land of the Ute and Apache and Navajo, a terrain created by powerful geologic forces and shaped by water. Its immense sky is broken only by shiny black ravens calling (in perfect English), "Rock! Rock! Rock!"

Carved in the rock near my home on the very edge of the Colorado Plateau are mountain sheep, spirals, stars, and various-sized bear paws complete with long scratchy claws. Someone from the Noochew (Ute) tribe was the artist, long ago. The Noochew, like their distant relatives the Numa (Southern Paiute), are among the more recent peoples of the Plateau, along with the Diné (Navajos) and the Tindé (Apache). It's generally believed that these groups began to make their way to this area at about the same time the Puebloans and Fremont began to disappear, 700 to 800 years ago. Because these more recent groups are still residents here, we know more about their cultures and languages.

The Ute and Southern Paiute people are related linguistically, speaking Numic languages, a branch of the Uto-Aztecan family. Interestingly enough, the nearby Hopi and more distant Mexican

Tarahumara Indians also speak languages belonging to this linguistic family, indicating a long-ago common ancestry.

Thinking of what my friend Antonio said, I wonder if I wouldn't have to learn Ute to adequately describe this landscape of the Noochew. But I suspect that only a native speaker could really understand all the language's nuances, someone who grew up in the Ute culture. Antonio also tells me that Ute speakers have only one word for blue and green and all shades between.

The Navajo and Apache languages are related to one another, both branches of the Athabaskan (Na-Dené) family, which claims cousins in California and far-away Canada. Lipan Apache, once spoken on the Mescalero Reservation in New Mexico, no longer has any living speakers. The Chiricahua Apache dialect has only one word for the colors blue, green, and turquoise.

Back at camp now, I take the small piece of quartz from my pocket and hold it up to the sun. That nameless color is still there, that bluish-white-rose—or did I just give it a name?

Are some languages more suitable for speaking of nature? Are Apache and Navajo somehow intrinsically "wilder" than English? Wouldn't it make sense that those languages whose speakers are historically closer to the land have a richer lexicon for speaking of things such as the scent of water floating before the thunderstorm?

If we listen, our Apache and Navajo and Ute friends tell us, the land and its creatures will speak to us. Stories of vision quests are rich with such language, and the seeker commonly takes on the name of the animal that spoke to him, whether by touch or through vision. But we must listen. The pinyon trees speak their own language, they speak of changing shadows as the sun moves through its arc in the desert sky.

We speak of the natural world, and Nature may speak to us, but for many Native Americans, one of the most important tasks of language is to speak to the land through prayer and thanksgiving:

We Are Singing in the Night

Now as the night is over us we are singing the songs that were given to us.

You see the clouds beginning to form on top of the mountains.

They look like little white feathers.

You will see them shake like feathers in the wind.

Soon the raindrops will fall and make our country beautiful.[1]

If the Spaniards had spent more time listening when they came to the New World, listening to the land and its peoples, they would have learned much. They brought with them a new material culture and religion, and they also brought a new language, and with it a different way of seeing the world, a different set of sensory filters. The attempt to impose these onto an ancient and unified culture finally led to the Spaniards' downfall—the Pueblo Revolt.

But the Spaniards weren't the only ones who wanted to impose their language and ways on the people of the Southwest. Our government programs for many years forbade the native children from speaking their own tongues, removing them to government schools and punishing them for not assimilating into our culture. And only recently have we begun to listen, to realize how much has been lost.

It's evening now, and as I lean against a warm chunk of sandstone covered with dry lichen, I watch a satellite as it glides silently through a black field of night sprinkled with stars, then disappears behind high cirrus clouds. Lower, gliding effortlessly, a jetliner flashes its red and white lights. Leaning back in their seats and eating dinner, the passengers are watching a documentary on water buffalo. As deep night falls, this landscape surrounding me now tells me to be still and listen. The stars are singing.

Without language we could not retain a complete or coherent picture of the physical world, says our Western scientific tradition. Linguists are a bit defensive when it comes to what we call "impressions" and "musings," and rightly so, for our discipline requires that we methodically and rigorously match data and hypothesis. But can we still trust our own senses?

The nineteenth-century French linguist Ferdinand de Saussure stood linguistics on its head when he spoke of language as an organic, living system, a web of interrelated meanings. It was not a mechanical and structural construct that we could easily relegate to a dictionary and set of rules. And, he said, this web is continually evolving and changing.

Since then, the field of linguistics has tried hard to bridge the chasm between the intuitive and the scientifically verifiable, between how we feel when we speak and what actually happens on a physical level. Because our tool for analysis is the very tool we're analyzing, we have long been constrained by the very thing we wish to understand.

But now, with the assistance of "brain microscopes," neuro-linguists are beginning to look deep into the human brain to comprehend speech activity. They are asking questions about what occurs in the brain when we hear a word—and what happens when we hear sounds that are not language, but are similar to it, such as musical tones.

The magnetoencephalogram, or MEG, is an imaging system that detects minute magnetic fields and gives extremely precise information on the brain's electrophysiology. This sensitive (and expensive) machine, which is even more precise than the MRI, is being used to test theories of language and the brain.

For example, when people create sentences, they are following codes of mental grammar, and in the process are performing complex computational operations—instantly and effortlessly. Comparing brain waves between word and sentence utterances, the MEG can provide clues to whether or not words have similar intricate internal structures. If so, brain activity will have the same patterns within a word as within a sentence, though more compressed in time.

Such studies will hopefully shed light on the relationship between language and cognition, providing insight into how humans differ from animals. It has long been thought that linguistic intelligence is found in the left side of the brain, in the planum temporale, which is on the upper surface of the temporal lobe. But a recent study shows that this area is nearly as well developed in chimpanzees. Perhaps this region of the brain has been over-rated—or perhaps chimps have a form of language that we have yet to recognize, maybe one with more emphasis on the senses and their immediate physical world.

Thinking again of color, I come back to my piece of quartz, still in my pocket after these many days. Why don't Apache and Ute have numerous terms for the colors of the sky, the water, the colors of azurite and malachite? Why don't Zuni speakers have words to distinguish between yellow and orange?

Languages have a multitude of ways for dealing with color. The language of the Shawnee (who live in Oklahoma) has a morpheme (one of the basic building blocks of a language) that is used with color terms to express a color for which no lexical item exists. For example, a Shawnee speaker would use the term "skipakya" to describe the color blue, and the term "halem-skipakya" for the color green. This "halem" morpheme also precedes the word for red in order to express the color brown.

In Omaha-Ponca (spoken by Siouan Indians, once enemies of the Utes) color terms may depend on the distance one is from the object or on the clarity of the object. A modifier may be used to indicate a precise shade, such as "ppe'zittu" (grass+blue) for "green." Lakhota Sioux uses different words for color depending on whether something is painted, dyed, or personal (like eyes or hair). It also often uses the term "elk-colored" to describe things.

Linguists have long been fascinated with the color systems of languages. Puzzled as to why some languages have only two terms (warm, cool) for the entire range of colors represented by English red, yellow, orange, blue, green, and purple, some thought that such languages represented different conceptualizations by their speakers.

Anthropologists and linguists alike began to ask in the early part of the twentieth century if it might be possible for language to actually shape cognition. Is it possible that, as a Lakhota speaker, the medium for creating the color is more important to me than the color itself? And color is only one of many areas in which languages differ. For example, many languages categorize things differently. Navajo-speaking children are more likely to group things together on the basis of shape than are English-speaking children.

Can the new brain-scanning techniques help answer the question of how language relates to thought? Perhaps, although it's too soon to tell. There is evidence that language can influence brain capacity. Studies indicate that the neural bases of human language and thought form a complex network of circuits within and connecting the structures of the brain. There exist critical periods in a child's life when the brain is biologically best equipped to learn language—when the brain's capacity actually is determined by the degree of language and learning to which a child is exposed.

According to MEG studies, each child has more than 50,000 nerve pathways that can carry sounds from the voice to the brain. The brain encodes words and actually rearranges its brain cells into connections to produce language. If a child hears little or no speech, the brain will eventually retire these cells, giving them a different function. By age 10, if the child has heard no spoken words, the ability to learn spoken language is lost. And between the ages of 4 and 12 an enormous amount of brain restructuring takes place, as the brain decides whether or not to keep a connection. If a child is receiving rich sensory stimulation, a surge of learning takes place.

Perhaps my vision of that quartz would be the same as my friend Antonio's only if we were both exposed to a rich linguistic environment as children. De Saussure's continually evolving web may be more accurate than his colleagues could have guessed. And learning another language may open our boundaries to new ways of looking at the world, just as exploring the natural world opens new boundaries of the senses. We linguists may exhibit admirable skill in analyzing languages, but even the least astute among us knows there is a dimension that simply can't be relegated to rules of structure and syntax.

From deep down in the age-old earth
clear waters appeared
a spring opened
and joined word to word.[2]

My endless questions have taken me back to my friend Antonio, and he and I are now bouncing along in my old Jeep through southern Utah, dodging sand dunes filtered across the road by autumn winds.

Radio voices come from the distance, from deep in the dark, speaking a language that seems as mysterious to us as the night wind carrying it.

Crackle…"Tséghahoodzání"…crackle…"Tuba City Ford damóo yázhí"…

As the voices disappear into static, I picture soundwaves floating over and down and around the buttes and canyons and hoodoos between here and Tuba City Ford.

Radio signal strengthens. "Ya'at'eeh. You're listening to the Voice of the Navajo Nation, KTTN, in Window Rock, Arizona, at 660 AM."

I can see the outline of Navajo Mountain against the night sky in the south, down towards where the Navajo-speaking DJ is sitting in front of his microphone in the broadcasting office of KTTN.

As the old Jeep sings gladly along on the flat straight road, bouncing on washboards, I ask, "Antonio, do you know any Navajo?"

"Not to speak of," he grins, then adds, "I bet the Japanese wish they'd learned Navajo."

"One of life's ironies," I comment. The U.S. government tried to extinguish the Navajo language, and yet we probably would have lost World War II if they'd been successful. The Navajo Code Talkers played a major role in our Pacific victory.

I turn off the radio, and we ride into the unchanging black-brush horizon, watered only by mirage clouds. Antonio continues, "You know, I don't speak my own tongue, the Nuchi, as well as I'd like. I learned some from my parents when I was young, but now I'm one of the lost children, as the grandparents call those of us who can't speak the old language. I no longer remember the song of the land."

He continues. "If I were to ask my own people, 'Um aa' nuu apag'ad? Do you speak Ute?' Most would say, 'kuch, no.' Fewer and fewer of my people speak the old tongue. It's sad. Our culture, our traditions, go hand in hand with our language—it's all intertwined."

I ask quietly, "What is lost when a language is lost?"

The truck drones on, and we pass a sign that says "Watch for Eagles on Highway." After a long time, Antonio answers, "You can't force the Indian back into someone, and once a language is gone, then so are those things that reflect who we are—our greetings to one another, our songs, our cures, our prayers, our wisdom. My mother spoke Ute to me when she was dying, but I couldn't understand her. But we must also look beyond ourselves—the voice of the land is in our language."

"You make me think of Fernado Pessoa, the Portuguese poet, who said, 'My homeland is the Portuguese language.'"

"Maybe he understands," Antonio replies, "and maybe I can still be Ute without the language, be Ute in English, but it's not the same. I can say in English, 'I rode my horse today,' and you can easily picture me on the horse, but do you feel the wind on your face, hear the three-point cadence of the gallop, feel the warmth against your legs, like when I speak of the horse in Ute? Of course it's not all language, you have to know the tradition of the horse, a thing also passing from my people."

Antonio pauses, then adds, smiling, "Last year my sister took our great-grandparents' Indian-agency-assigned last name, Duncan, to a genealogist. She was told that we're related to Queen Mary of Scotland."

The Ute language is not alone—perhaps as many as half of the world's languages are dying or at risk (there are currently around 6,700 languages spoken worldwide). Our neighbor tongue here in the southwest, Havasupai, is listed as endangered by the Linguistic Society of America, as are many dialects of Keresan (including Acoma, San Felipe, Santa Ana, and Santo Domingo), that ancient tongue possibly spoken by some of the Ancestral Puebloans themselves.

But the native people of the Colorado Plateau are fighting to save their languages. The Southern Utes' language and culture program has become a model for other tribes. The Hopis have just completed an official dictionary. The Navajos are continuing efforts to get the native language used in public and boarding schools on the reservation. The Tohono O'odham language is seeing a resurgence of interest, as well as a dictionary in progress. The University of Northern Arizona teaches the Navajo language, and the College of Eastern Utah teaches Ute.

Many religious traditions tell us that a diversity of languages is a good thing. According to the Acoma Pueblo Indians, people were meant to speak different languages so that it's not easy for them to argue. Among the Navajo, language is the means through which the world is created, organized, classified, and beautified. Dewey Healing, a Tewa, writes, "How far will we carry forth our Tewa Language, we elders, as we live our days?"

Too many indigenous peoples are watching their languages pass—from spoken to grave, with but a moment between. When the elders, those who speak that tongue as their primary language, are gone, the language is, in essence, lost, at least in its original dimensions. Thus the urgency. Like an endangered species, the world is less without each language—we have lost a thread to our own humanness.

Dead languages do not evolve and change, and new languages cannot be born of dead dialects. Often entire systems of sacred religious terms are lost, for these are rarely recorded in dictionaries. Once a language is extinct, it becomes words on paper, like a stuffed condor in a museum. And we all lose, for when we immerse ourselves in the study of other languages, of other cultures, we become recipients of new ways of thinking, of new thought pathways, perhaps even of new colors. Without this, our human diversity is lessened. We forget the song of the land, we forget who we are.

Night deepens, and a small cluster of lights comes into view, a mile or so off to the left of the road. The desert now seems lonely, with this small reminder of humankind.

Old decrepit buildings mark the block-long town. Smell of burning juniper. Antonio lives in a small shack on the edge, surrounded by tall greasewood, giving it some sense of shelter from the desert's cold open arms.

Antonio opens the Jeep door and gets out, leaning through the open window, and says, "My fourth-grade nephew, a bright student, was given an English assignment by his non-native teacher to write a one-page expository essay on autumn in the mountains. He was baffled when the teacher told him he'd failed."

"What did he write?" I ask.

Antonio speaks quietly, "All his essay said was, 'Autumn is a million colors floating in the air.'"

Softly I answer, "He is learning the song of the land."

Antonio smiles, then is gone.

---

1. Tohono O'odham poem from Francis Densmore, Papago Music, BAE, Bulletin 90.
2. The Russian poet Oktyabrina Voronova, in Voronova 1996: 103; transl. by Pekka Sammallahti.

Urban Nature: Your Place or Mine

Penelope Grenoble O'Malley

THERE IS A PLACE on the eastbound Ventura Freeway, between the Haskell Boulevard off-ramp and the 101/405 interchange, where if you're stopped in traffic in the far right lane, next to the concrete-block wall that protects the houses next to the freeway from the roar of thousands of cars going seventy miles an hour, and if it's January or February and it's just rained—so the dust and smog haven't had a chance to rise yet—you can look out your driver's side window, past the roofs of the cars to your left, and see nothing but the Santa Susana Mountains.

You won't see the ticky-tacky grid of houses that stretches for six miles between the freeway and those mountains or the nondescript glass-and-chrome office buildings, the thrown-together corner malls, or the Anglo churches with the extra line of Spanish or Filipino letters stenciled above the door. Instead you will look right past the wire-mesh fence mounted on top of the concrete K-rail on the far side of the freeway and see only mountains and blue sky and green grass. If you're lucky, like I was the day I am talking about, the first day I noticed this, with traffic stopped because a slide blocked Pacific Coast Highway in Malibu and the morning's commuters all crowded onto the freeway, you might also see a red-tailed hawk circling the thin strip of grass, looking for a mouse or a rabbit.

Or maybe there will be two hawks, and if you're lucky there'll be snow on the San Gabriel Mountains in the east quadrant of your view, and you will look out your car window and think, "I could be in New Mexico or Arizona, out where they shoot the Patagonia catalogue, where they take the photographs for the wildlife calendars." But you're not. You're in Los Angeles, with 10 million other people and eight other freeways, most of them bumper to bumper at this hour, even though at the moment you don't feel it. What you feel are the hawk and whatever the hawk is hunting in the green field next to the freeway, and this makes you wonder, Is this enough?

Is this image enough, the knowledge that there's raw land under the freeway and at any time that land could rear up, like it did eight years ago when the earth shook and pushed the mountains I'm looking at a foot closer to the sky? Is it enough that the field is there and the hawk and whatever the hawk is scouting? Will the image hold until I can get out to where they take the photographs, out where I can clamp on a pair of snowshoes and skim across ten inches of new snow? And why does this image make me tingle? Because this small strip of land is the way it's supposed to be, free and unencumbered, the possibilities unpredictable? Because the land exists this way and the hawk, hemmed in by concrete and threatened by too many people, is still here and still real?

Like the canyon behind my house is real, where I can walk for five miles due north and not see another person, even though I know there is a line of subdivisions on the other side of the canyon wall and a four-lane highway and two shopping centers?

Where I can sit on a battered gray picnic table under an old oak close to my house and look northwest and see nothing but open hills and rolling oak savanna—it's another one of those calendar views. Until one day I think, "There are houses on the other side of those hills," and this makes me wonder about those calendar shots, about what might actually be to the right or left of the sharp-peaked mountain in the photographs I admire, the quiet lake that appears so serene. When I am thinking like this I begin to suspect whoever took those shots of some fine points of manipulation, presenting something that might not really exist because whoever took the photographs knows what I want to see: infinite nature. Isolated, distant. Thinking this way gets me wondering how much nature I really need, how much land and how perfect it has to be, and what I need it for.

There are signs marking the placement of underground pipelines every mile or so along the first half of the trail I hike into my canyon: Caution, High Pressure Gas Line and Warning: Petroleum Pipe Line. The signs march down one side of the canyon and up the other and up and down the canyon next door and the canyon after that. The petroleum sign is black and yellow, round like an old gasoline pump, but the sign for the high-pressure gas line is rectangular and white, and on bright afternoons, when the sun is at just the right angle, light reflects off the burnished metal. On days like that, when my gaze is drawn to the yellow and green of spring mustard lying like plush on the hills, I look up and notice the reflected light and wonder what's up there. Then I remember: the pipeline signs.

I know if I walk high enough on the west side of my canyon, I will see the road and the walled subdivisions on the other side. I forced myself to do that one day because I don't want to be fooled. I want my experience of the canyon to correspond to what I know is real. I have seen where the pipelines cross the stream in the canyon bottom, slung on supports above the ground like a miniature Golden Gate Bridge. The pipelines and the metal poles they're suspended on are painted a too-pink shade of beige, which doesn't blend with the dusty color of the dried grasses that blanket the canyon bottom in summer and stands out even worse against the waxy green leaves of new season oaks. In the same way the hills hide the subdivisions behind the canyon's far wall, I know if I stand in the right place on the small rise where the dirt road comes in from the canyon next door, I won't see the maintenance yard the water company keeps here in the canyon or the cinder-block wall that encloses the gas tanks that are stored there. What I will notice is the way the land rises steadily toward the abandoned sheep pasture known as Shepherds' Flat. Likewise I know that when I reach Shepherds' Flat, my attention will be focused on the high sandstone ridge that rises to the north and not on the Rocketdyne test lab I know is located behind the ridge. I am aware the lab is there because I was out walking one day when they fired up a jet engine. At first I thought it was an airplane taking off, until I realized the sound didn't diminish like the whine of jet engine does when an aircraft leaves the ground.

If I am complacent and forget these things are part of the canyon, I will become agitated and disappointed when they turn around and bite me. Like the Saturday morning the engine whine first distracted me, when I was tracing the pattern water had left beside the trail from a storm the night before, or another time when I stood watching a hawk land on the nest it had anchored to the steel girders of a power line tower. Or the day I was being particularly careful about where I put my feet because it was April and the rattlers were out and baby rattlesnakes don't know about controlling their venom. I want to stay current. I want to remember these things are part of the canyon. I don't want the pipeline signs and the jet engine noise to catch me off-guard in the act of thinking I'm somewhere else, out where they shoot the Patagonia catalogues and the wildlife calendars.

If by "perfect" I mean "wild" in the sense of uninhabited (by humans in the present tense) and unfettered with streetlights or sidewalks, or a place where I can't predict what might happen (a bobcat, normally a shy and reclusive animal, crossing my trail in broad daylight), then I guess I'm okay thinking of my canyon as wild. But if by wild I mean uncivilized, my canyon is far from perfect. Until a decade ago herds of cattle cut trails across its fragile hillsides and trampled its soft riparian bottom. The hills still bear the scars of their hooves, and the canyon floor is littered with weeds and introduced plants that took hold once the soil was disturbed. The trail I hike is actually a dirt road with fences and cattle guards built along its length. Uphill from the old ranch site, from which debris scatters downcanyon when enough wind blows from the right direction, a wide gash in the chaparral tells me where a water main is buried. Plus my canyon has been broken to human purpose in another way. Even with all its scars it has been rescued from a speculator's dream of a golf course and two thousand "fairway" homes ("Go out to where the houses stop," Bob Hope advised Southern California investors. "Buy land."), and it now emits a sacrosanct quality, redeemed at the hands of Hope's neighbors, who were determined to keep what wilderness remains here, because wild, even urban wild, gives pleasure to the senses and to the spirit. On good days, when the jet engines are quiet and I pass the pipeline signs without noticing them, when my eye is caught by the purple and green of spring lupine, my canyon does indeed have the power to exalt the mind.

How much land do I need and what do I need it for? Do I need the land, actually, or only the knowledge that the land is there? Space or a photograph that suggests vastness set apart? "Open space," as we say in the cities, an area with distance and volume, an expanse of breadth and width and depth, a wild sweep without houses and malls and office parks, valuable because it separates us from what we ourselves have created. Not empty space, because empty implies something in need of filling. Certainly not unoccupied—by people, yes, but not if you think of possums and rattlesnakes, bobcats and cougars. One night after she'd had a glass of wine, a woman I ride with in the canyon suggested the park service should remove the cougars that live hereabouts because unlike us, visitors don't know there are cougars in the canyon and cougars can be dangerous. Is it true people don't know the difference between a small strip of grass next to the freeway and an entire canyon set apart like ours? Is it true they don't know that to live comfortably, a cougar needs thirty thousand acres to roam? A few days ago, running along the canyon bottom, I surprised two hikers, not hikers actually, a man and a woman in street shoes. The man grinned. "I thought you were a bear."

"Haven't seen a deer yet this year," I shouted, attempting to set him straight on the local fauna.

"You mean there's deer out there?"

I told him yes, there were deer out here. I was about to add "and coyotes and bobcats," but I let it go at the deer.

⌒

Some people say they need space and lots of it so they can feel free. But free from what? The artificial constraints of civilization, as one rancher put it, the crowds and the compromises, an area big enough and open enough to feel safe from outsiders, an out-of-the-way place. But out of the way of what? A place to burrow in, where every day you see mountains and you don't have to wait for a lucky chance on the freeway when the traffic stops. Putting distance, enormous distance, between yourself and the rest of us, ah, that's perfection.

I hear some people look for solace in nature, to minimize grief or anxiety. What's the idea here? You look at the mountains, imagine a grizzly ripping open the side of a salmon, and all's right with the world? And if not now, soon? Some people say they find comfort in the order they find in nature. In the middle of what doesn't make sense in their lives, they find a reasonableness that's reassuring. Others say they connect with something in the silence the wind blows their way; they imagine life on that picture-perfect mountain is simpler than what batters them day-to-day. There is also nature as adventure, as a way to test oneself, like the mountain bikers who ride at night in my canyon dodging April rattlesnakes. Other people hope what they experience in nature will bring out the best in them, that the sight of the San Gabriel Mountains with a dusting of snow will stir inner resources. Living in that faraway place, out of sight of the rest of the world for a week or a year or a lifetime, some people say they come to terms with themselves, with life at its most primitive. Some people say nature is a place to find God. "Live in the moment," they say, like the grizzly with its salmon, like the coyote stealing Pringles from my garbage can. Live in the moment and feel yourself connected with the web of life. Given this kind of awakening, a small patch of open land next to the freeway becomes sacred, as removed from what is real as the converted are from the rest of us.

Have you noticed the common denominator, the reference point? It's us. Are we running from each other, do you think, or do we yearn to be outside ourselves, to be part of something larger? It's a good deal to ask from a small patch of open ground next to the freeway or a sharp granite ridge. And what is it that we bring to the party? Only ourselves it seems, loaded down with both enthusiasm and angst.

Isak Dinesen said it: "There is no world without Nairobi's streets." Recalling life on the East African frontier, Dinesen understood the value of human company, its worth, say, compared to standing in sight of a lion. More than one biologist has said it: We are driven to conquer even as we fear the loss of what is distant and unknown and mysterious. A poet in a workshop in Moab, Utah said it: "I never thought of apple trees as nature."

Could it be the value of wild places is how they stand in contrast to what we humans have made, and our job then is to bear witness? We build our houses to take advantage of the view. Los Angeles from the Hollywood Hills suggests the vastness of a rolling sea. In the California desert, writer and naturalist Mary Austin sought a place where her "creature instincts" might grow, where she could find "room enough and time enough." Might there be solace in Austin's distant place, the sense of satisfaction of connecting spirit close to body and both to one peculiar patch of ground? (In my canyon there is not quite room enough. If I have the dogs with me, I also have to watch for the ranger's truck; it's fifty dollars if he catches me with the border collies off leash.)

"Perhaps I don't like the idea that we humans have taken over," I scribble on the open page of book I'm reading. "I don't like that once we get a taste of something, we always want more than we need." There's a fence around the acre my husband and I call home. Even in April I walk around the yard barefoot, as if the fence will keep the rattlesnakes out. "This is my territory," I say to the snakes. "This is where we have coffee in the morning, where we sit with guests on Saturday nights. Your place is in the grass across the street."

Like most people, I am susceptible to images. Given a good sturdy mountaintop bathed in sundown light, I lose whatever capacity I have to think critically. The image becomes the test of what is real, the yardstick by which to measure the value of actual experience. And the image is always perfect, which is what we count on. "It was right out of Nature (the TV show) my husband tells me, describing the four-foot rattler he spotted near the entrance to our canyon. Having seen a real rattlesnake for himself, he didn't think that TV got it right—captured the essence of rattlesnake. Instead the television image became the benchmark by which he assessed the authenticity of his own encounter.

Across the Santa Monica Mountains from where I live, real estate agents have invented the Queen's Necklace to sell ridge-top houses, a half-circle of shoreline lights that stretches from Malibu to Redondo Beach and on clear nights to the hump of Palos Verdes. Without an uncluttered mountaintop close at hand or a nice patch of empty desert, will the Queen's Necklace do, token of infinity of another kind? Never mind that what lies beneath this pleasant arrangement of sparkling lights is what many of us run from: all those people. Never mind that the openness of the ocean, the blackness the necklace outlines, the image we can't see, is what we're really after.

I used to keep an Ansel Adams calendar in my office, the kind you hang on the wall, with a photograph on top and the days of the month lined up in a grid underneath. Last year I exchanged Adams's landscapes for a set of flower portraits by Georgia O'Keeffe. I thought at first I wanted to keep company with a woman; then I realized I was off experimenting again—how much image is enough? I thought O'Keeffe's tight focus might replace the sweep of an Adams landscape, now that I know how easily I can be fooled, what a little judicious cropping can do. I thought I might learn something from thinking on the level of cells and molecules for a change, bonding with life at a more elemental level. But I selected the wrong model. O'Keeffe's work is first of all about form. The depth of her witness crops out the clutter, true, but the detail adds perspective more intensely than a camera's shutter. Did I really want that on my wall? Much easier to glance over and see Half Dome familiar in its cloak of snow and ice.

One day in May I turned to check the date, caught O'Keeffe's Light Iris in my peripheral vision and got nothing. I had to stop what I was doing and focus full attention on the flower. Right away I noticed how easily I could sight past the petals of the domineering flower to the shapeless pink-gray-green background, then how the petals curved downward from the center of the painting in a way that evoked the depth of a subterranean cave. One small dark-green triangle suggested an abyss. I began thinking how static those landscape photographs are, the perfect moment captured. I decided Light Iris is about process: in O'Keeffe's portrayal of the lush world of this single flower—no stem, no leaves—lies its imminent decay. Adams's photographs remind me of what I know. O'Keeffe's flowers point me to a place I have never been before. And in the act of sliding forward into O'Keeffe's abyss, I understand that it is not only space which matters, but also what that space contains, the way a piece of land functions—how it drains and feeds itself, its cycles of propagation, birth, decay—and how important you are, the woman whose horse I borrow on Tuesday mornings, the friend I'm meeting for drinks on Friday. If I didn't have you, would I be so anxious to escape to that distant mountaintop, so keen to see a cougar? Over dinner or a glass of wine, I talk, swap ideas. In the canyon, I am quiet. I collect what I can, come home and lasso my experience with pen on paper, can't wait to speak with you about what I've seen.

The small size of the rattler's head surprised me. Poking up between the coils of the garden hose in rigid S-like motion, the head said baby. Once the hose was moved, I saw the body was adolescent and growing up fast. "Look," said my husband, as the snake burrowed back among the coils. "You can't see the son-of-a-bitch," as if the snake were being intentionally menacing.

So it has happened, what my husband feared. April, fence or no fence, our territory or not, a baby rattler coiled three feet from the teak table where we eat our summer dinners, three steps away from my office slider. How much space do we need? How much room is enough? However much territory this snake claimed, it fell short. I thought we might leave it where it was, but my husband reminded me of the dogs. He rummaged around in the garage for a shovel and before I realized what he was doing, he slammed the blade through the snake's body and scooped up the severed parts. I stood there a minute, remembering that a rattler's head can bite up to an hour after it's been severed, then started after him to see what he was doing with the remains. Our house is one of the last before the unbuilt land that leads into the canyon. When I couldn't find the snake in the garbage can, I walked to the end of the driveway and turned north up the street just in time to see my husband carry the severed parts over to the road and dump the rattler in the dry summer grass on the other side, back where it belonged.

Are They More Moral in Montana?

Penelope Grenoble O'Malley

ABOUT THREE YEARS AGO I developed the habit of reading the notes about contributors in the front of magazines. Not all magazines, mind you; mostly those with an environmental slant or concerned with what when I was a kid I would have called "the outdoors." Even knowing the idea is to strike the right chord and come off sounding successful and interesting, I still get chills when I read about some writer who lives on a remote island off the coast of British Columbia or someone else who showers in water heated by wood she's split herself, or worse, a woman who homesteaded a ranch in the Rockies—Wyoming or maybe Montana. I'm not even clear about what homesteading involves, but when I hear that special combination of high mountains and sparse population, I get a sinking feeling in the pit of my stomach. "I could be out there," I think— chopping wood, hunting elk. "I should be out there."

I am immoral, I chastise myself, certain that my life in gas-guzzling, land-grabbing Southern California sanctions behavior I find both offensive and self-defeating. I lack courage. A little over-wrought, you say. Perhaps. But it happens every time I read one of those magazine bios, and often enough in between. Am I part of the problem? Could I be part of the solution?

I want what I do to be well founded. I want to live responsibly. In Montana or Wyoming or Idaho, I might be inspired to partic-

ipate in the natural order of things. I might experience a break-
through, become an example to others, repair the moth holes that
threaten to unravel the fabric of my life. In Montana, I might recover from the wounds I've sustained living in the city, the constant
disease I suffer. City life can be difficult, brutal. Life in the city can
make you bitter. Life out there in Montana or Wyoming looks a
lot kinder, out where nature prevails. In Montana I might
develop perspective. My life would be principled in the sense that
I could do my part, making good with the space and time I've
been allocated.

Standing on the corner of Highland Boulevard and Franklin
Avenue in Hollywood staring up at the billboards, I get the scoop
on Sony's latest CD player, I learn about the latest made-for-TV
movie. Smelling the exhaust, jostled by two women walking arm and
arm, I feel a twinge of excitement: I'm happy to be here. Here where
things are happening. These days the experience is infrequent. I live
outside the city now, past the farthest of LA's far-out suburbs. I
come into town only occasionally, tonight for the premiere of a
friend's play. But Hollywood is old turf. I edited the West Coast's
largest underground newspaper in Hollywood, laid out copy in a
warehouse with walls painted black and telephone cords dangling
from the ceiling. I spent Saturday nights photographing prostitutes
on Hollywood Boulevard, went to rallies with hippie hero Jerry
Rubin, sat in Hank Bukowski's living room talking poetry and
drinking beer. Later, I edited film in an office four blocks south of
where I'm standing. Are these activities immoral, do you think,
needing, as they do, a city to sustain them? And does this mean I've
mislaid the impulse I came west to fulfill?

I, too, dreamed of a cabin in the redwoods, a kitchen garden,
acres of my own land to stroll or till. Watching a mother in a sundress

and two children in Tide-clean T-shirts push a shopping cart around a supermarket in Culver City, the screwball Hollywood scenes I encountered daily flashed in front of me. At least here, in this part of town, things are normal. Also in Montana.

I have lived in half a dozen neighborhoods since I moved to Southern California: a town house there in Culver City (swimming pool and Jacuzzi), a "modest" postwar bungalow near Beverly Hills, a glass aviary in Bel Air, a ranch house in Malibu. Each time I thought I had what I wanted, but each move was in fact an attempt to edge further out of town. Now I've fooled around long enough. It's time to pack my bags, time to head for Montana.

And what will I do once I get there? I imagine I will have more time for things that matter. In Montana I will compost my garbage and recycle what's left. I will plant a garden, cook with the seasons, can what I don't eat. I will have more energy to convince my husband to build a solar house or a rammed earth house or a house made of straw bales, more time to watch the stars and take long walks in uncluttered landscapes. In Montana, nobody will care what I look like. I will raise sheep and buy my clothes at Wal-Mart.

And how will my defection aid Southern California? To start with, there would be one less car on the freeway (two, counting my husband's, although not having consulted him, I'm not sure how he'll take to the idea), two less cars adding to the congestion and traffic, the noise and the smog. One less person taking clothes to the dry cleaner, two less people consuming energy—forced air in the winter, air-conditioning in the summer—one less lawn guzzling water and water-polluting fertilizer, three less cans of yard waste added to the dump. Untold less dog droppings on the street.

And if not Montana, where? Where would I go if my husband suddenly declared himself ready to leave? "Olancha," I think. "Catalina." "Acton." Olancha in the Owens Valley, on the eastern edge of the Sierras, acres of flat land and church barbecues where I'd meet my (distant) neighbors. Catalina Island, twenty-six miles across the sea from LA's noise and bustle, where I'd hike up a ridge to watch the winter sun set and cheer the Fourth of July parade on its half-mile run down the island's main street. In Acton, perched on the edge of the Mojave Desert, I'd wait out the winter listening to the wind sweep across my parched acres, dreaming of the poppies and lupine that blanket the hillsides each spring. I could step into each of these places ready-made and wait patiently to bloom.

To be fair, I have set myself up here as best I can. I live down the street from four thousand acres of parkland that will never be developed. I can run, ride a horse, or walk the dogs for ten miles straight without seeing a house or, most days, another person. The neighborhood goes back to the first settlement in this valley; you can still see the bones of the old farmhouses under layers of modern renovations. The houses snake up and down the hills, following the contour of the land. The houses are all different—no gates, no streetlights, no security patrol. So what's the problem? Why Montana? The problem is the nervous strain that comes with LA's particular kind of urban-suburban living, the fact that I can't walk anywhere, that I shop by driving from one mall or plaza or center to another, that the nearest of my longtime friends is forty minutes away at seventy miles an hour, that there are so many of us strung out in suburbs and perched on knobby hilltops, stuffed into nooks and crannies wherever we can find enough room to draw a breath.

One other thing while I'm being frank: I came here under false pretenses. I wanted out of the East, where the land having been brought to heel, the remaining challenges seemed cerebral. I wanted out of the false sophistication—and the bad weather. On a visit to the West Coast before I made the final bolt across the continent, I took home images of high-rolling Pacific waves, golden hills that dropped straight to the sea, the scent of orange blossoms. Standing in the sun outside the old Spanish-style building that was then LA's airport terminal, only a narrow metal tube between me and home, I could just as well have stayed. And what did I remember about the city itself? Not much. The old Ambassador Hotel, already lurching toward seedy, my aunt's "garden apartment" on Catalina Street. The Hollywood sign.

Why don't I leave? Don't know, can't say. Although I could tell you about the day I drove south through the rolling country between San Luis Obispo and Buelton, above Santa Barbara. At first it all looked solid and comforting, the small family ranches connected by grassy bottomland and oak-covered hills. Then I noticed how much development had occurred in the ten years since I'd been there last. A countryside that once seemed the archetype of Southern California now appeared less fortifying. What once appeared as a limitless horizon of untamed landscape was now littered with settlement, private homes and horse ranches to be sure, but much more that was intrusive—subdivisions, strip malls, discount stores—so what open space remained seemed less authentic than I remembered, a throwback to a lesser time.

From the time we humans abandoned agriculture for towns, then towns for urban centers bustling with commerce and industry, we have thought of cities as the place to be. Cities are where things come together and thought is advanced, where art and culture develop and trends coalesce. Cities are where the action is. Driving through that open land north of Santa Barbara, seeing more and more of the rolling hills pockmarked with gated housing developments and industrial parks, I began to think of those small towns struggling to become cities not as progressive (no doubt the way they think of themselves), but backward actually, wet behind the ears. Knowing what has happened down south where I live, how silly to hold your hand out for more of the same: golf courses ringed with "estate" homes, wave after wave of franchised hotels and restaurants. I pictured the town oligarchy swelling with pride as the mayor or some beaming entrepreneur cut the ribbon on a new office building. "No grass growing under our feet." Enthusiastic signs announced I could expect more of the same. Good-bye oaks and grassland. H-e-l-l-o McDonalds.

Down where I live we are interested in progress of another sort. We consider ourselves kin to Californians of another era who addressed problems government couldn't or wouldn't handle. This time it's not better schools and more efficient water districts and nailing politicians grossly on the take, but quality of life, slow growth (now there's an oxymoron), and protecting what's left of what hasn't been developed.

Coming down the Calabasas Grade on the 101 freeway after lunch with a friend who lives in west Los Angeles, thinking about having a facelift (that's what I get for having friends in the city), thinking about injections and peels and whether or not I should get lifted—who would care—and whether it should be a full lift or just "a little work here and there," I am knocked off-kilter, my vision of tighter chin and wide-eyed look pitched off-balance by a gash in a normally unblemished hillside. The graded cut off to my right is a half mile long and vaguely elliptical. The protective cover of spring grass has been ripped off, the underlying soil exposed. "Now what?" I think. "What else do I have to worry about?"

The 101 freeway heading north is one of the most picturesque ways to leave Los Angeles. A few miles farther down the road things are more developed, but right there where the grade falls out of the packed-in neighborhoods of the San Fernando Valley, the landscape is more open, mostly because growth has been contained by much concerted effort on the part of citizens and a few dedicated government agencies. If I disregard the thin margin of office buildings along the freeway, I have a view of oak-covered foothills and the steep peaks of Malibu State Park, Lady Face Mountain in the distance. With less concrete to absorb the sun's radiation and little industry to promote traffic, the air temperature drops and the flow of cars begins to thin. On warm days in spring, fog rolls through Malibu Canyon from the beach, exhaling luminescent fingers against the valley's naked blue sky.

Driving along at a conservative sixty-five, thinking about the relative benefits of peels and lifts, remembering collagen works best but is temporary and I must be prepared for an annual investment of three thousand dollars, wondering if it should be a full lift or just a nip and tuck here and there, and do I really need a facelift (compared, say, to a new computer), and whamo, I get hit with this huge chunk of topsoil scrapped off the mountain. Yesterday, green hills; today, an ugly tear. As the road curves, I see the land at the eastern end of the wound no longer rolls like soft tissue but is flat and even, its edges tightly compacted and squared off at right angles. What's going on? What are they doing? You notice

I have already concluded that whoever they are they are up to no good (experience suggests that anytime someone takes a chunk out of a mountain, something bad is about to occur), and that I'm taking what's happening personally. Whoever it is that has cut that gash in the hill has not only despoiled my view but is stealing something valuable away from me. Isn't somebody going to do something?

Of course no one is doing anything. If they're grading, it's too late. But what I'm forfeiting is irreclaimable. It is not only my view of the way the hill curves, the soft cover of grass, the oak trees, it is the way the land feels under my feet. I have hiked up there on that slope. I have felt the calmness of that rolling landscape. I have breathed in the fertile scent of wet winter mornings, become tipsy with the scent of spring sage, felt the spirit of coyotes and bobcats, even cougars close upon the land. What they're doing is filling in a natural saddle to build a platform for a subdivision on an undisturbed hillside in the middle of a stand of ancient oaks. I'll be driving down that grade and right there as the freeway turns west there it will be: a tight, dense housing development, bright white houses with uniform red roofs jammed together with nothing but a few stumpy trees to break the glare and a white-washed cinder-block wall around the whole mess.

I am distraught, even desperate. And this is not all—listen to what else I have to contend with. Smack in the middle of the town where I live a developer is planning a shopping center that will be "anchored" by Target and The Home Depot. The new mall will front a quiet, tree-lined road that now wanders comfortably at two lanes but will have to be widened at the cost of thirteen full-grown oaks. The freeway interchange by which people will access this new mercantile emporium will have to be rebuilt ("streamlined" as both town officials and the developer describe it) so it looks like a labyrinth that would lead you astray in downtown Los Angeles. All this although there's a Home Depot ten minutes north on the freeway and two other discount home-improvement stores three and five minutes down the street. Literally next door to where The Home Depot is scheduled to sprawl once the oaks are removed is a long-established lumber yard and building supply store, another locally owned business that is doomed. At ground zero, a building equipment rental business has been serving local residents for over half a century. It, too, will have to move—or close.

Across the freeway from The Home Depot, another shopping center is scheduled to chew up six acres of open grassland. The developer insists he needs movie theaters to make the effort worthwhile, despite the eightplex struggling across the freeway. To build the theaters and provide enough parking and make it easier for people to get in and out, the hill that rises gracefully at the rear of the site will have to be leveled, exposing residents of the area's one remaining rural neighborhood to the lights and noise of urban Saturday nights. One freeway exit east, where a two-lane road wanders over a one-lane bridge into my neighborhood, a private school plans a satellite campus that will require taking down another hill and filling in a canyon bottom, plus upgrading another freeway ramp to accommodate mothers dropping off their darlings in the mornings. "Your community will have a place to meet," a representative of the school tells us when we protest. But we already have a place to meet, the riding arena across the street. The sign on the crossbar over the entrance to our neighborhood makes it clear where our priorities lie: "Old Agoura." Build your school someplace else.

At the end of the road I live on, just before it dead-ends into parkland, ninety acres of undeveloped oak savanna await their fate—ten houses or eight houses or six. Ten at least, says the developer, or he can't make good on his investment. When residents suggest the owner donate the land to the park that surrounds our neighborhood, his representatives fall back on scare tactics, warning that the park service is already considering a parking lot on the site if the land were to become available. You want that in your back-yard? I agree with my next-door neighbor. The landowner made a bad investment and now he wants the neighborhood to take up the slack. Tough you-know-what.

Ten years ago people laughed when their friends moved out here so far removed from the urban core of Los Angeles. The Conejo Valley was the boondocks. Twenty years ago there were sheep on the hills that now backdrop subdivisions; today we're growing four times faster than the rest of the country. Letters to the editor in the local newspapers fall evenly between saving open space and adding more restaurants and better shopping. Who wants to drive fifteen minutes to The Home Depot when a developer is prepared to install one in your own backyard? The politicians add their voices to the debate. Hamstrung by a rash of statewide initiatives from raising taxes, city councils are counting on sales tax revenue from new businesses to finance civic improvements, which in our case include a new library and a very elaborate city hall. For some of us this is sacred land, as close as we're likely to get to what we imagine in Montana. To others, it's comfortable housing at a reasonable price, good schools, a low crime rate. Who cares about Lady Face Mountain, the oaks along Agoura Road?

What else? Another shopping center, this one where the picturesque Calabasas Grade drops to the valley floor, a high-end shopping plaza with outlets like Barnes & Noble, which has already established branches eight minutes away in either direction.

"You other communities got yours," our neighbors insist. "We want ours." Right now, the land "theirs" will be built on supports a thriving community of native grasses and more of those aged oaks. The coup de grâce, the behemoth of them all, is Ahmanson Ranch, over three thousand homes, four hundred thousand square feet of commercial development, plus a hotel and two PGA golf courses on land that was originally zoned for thirty-four houses. Forty-six million cubic tons of dirt will have to be moved around, an effort that will take seven years. Some houses will be built on more than a hundred feet of fill.

No wonder Montana's so enticing. Until you remember that in Montana they have their own problems. Middle-aged yuppies with wide-eyed dreams of open space and hard-working immigrants from Southeast Asia for whom conservation is an unfamiliar concept. Streambeds eroded under the hooves of sheep and cattle, tailings from the halcyon days of mining endangering mountain streams, boomtowns gone bust and all the social problems that go along with this often-repeated western syndrome. Not to mention the overarching conflict between city folks arriving with distorted visions of rural life and those who have already established a life they consider just fine, thank you.

In any case, I've decided I can't leave. I've come to understand it's not so much the wear and tear of the city that makes me nervous— or the emotional strain of my personal moral ambiguity—but living always in the shadow of what might be taken from me, those inviting vistas, that open land I've come to depend on. I would take that fear with me to Montana. Do you imagine this is going to change? Do you imagine this "progress" is going to be halted? That it isn't headed for Montana? I can be part of the problem or part of the solution. Move to Montana and I become one of the statistics developers use to finance their Wal-Mart centers, their Home Depots. ("Look: another nut who wants to work with her hands.") In Montana, I'd just add to the problem, swell the ranks of refugees, help spread the disease. Besides, they don't want me in Montana. Better I stay put and do my part to find a solution here: stand by my neighbors, protest the school, document the "grass roots" organization that has been fighting the Ahmanson Ranch development for ten years. Ten years! There's the forward momentum I've been seeking. There's the progress: Stand and fight, take a crack at slaying the beast.

Do I imagine we'll stop it? Maybe not—probably not in time for me. But in time for Colorado maybe, and Idaho and Wyoming. In time for Montana. And maybe here also. In the ten years that grassroots group has been fighting the three thousand homes and two golf courses, it has also managed to save four thousand-plus undeveloped acres. It has stopped a road through a national park, fought another development scheduled for another fragile hillside, saved four hundred oak trees and a wetlands. To hell with Montana; I'm staying here!

A World Away

Leigh Calvez

THE CAPTAIN OF THE SIXTY-SEVEN-FOOT *OCEAN LIGHT* timed our arrival at British Columbia's Cornwall Inlet perfectly to coincide with the few moments when water neither rises nor falls—slack tide. Skillfully, Captain Eric Boyum threaded the boat's course through the narrow passage with only a few feet of water below the wooden hull. Tall spruce and lacy cedars sailed by, belted kingfishers dipped and soared, and long leaves of bull kelp swam like long brown hair blowing in the breeze.

It was day two of an eight-day adventure to Princess Royal Island along the north coast. With our leader, Dr. Chuck Jonkel, a bear biologist for forty-one years from the Great Bear Foundation, we—strangers, gathered simply by our love for bears—hoped to spot the rare white black bear. A holdover from the last ice age, this subspecies of black bear known as the Kermode or "Spirit Bear," inhabits only Princess Royal Island and a few surrounding islands and areas on the mainland. In recent years, it has become the "poster bear" for saving the last expanse of temperate rain forest in the world from logging.

For me this search for the spirit bear felt more like a search to find my own spirit. Over the last several months, my work as an environmental activist and nature writer had taken its toll. The current administration seemed to be throwing out hard-won environmental regulations on a daily basis, while threatening to open the Arctic National Wildlife Refuge to oil drilling. I raged against this lack of vision. As the U.S. Navy prepared to flood the world's oceans with enough loud, low-frequency sound to kill whales, dolphins, and other swimming creatures, I feared for the lives of the whales I had studied and loved. And when the secretary of the interior trashed the long-negotiated grizzly bear reintroduction plan for the Selway Bitterroot Ecosystem between Idaho and Montana, I felt defeated. Then one day, I found myself talking about the deaths of seven of Puget Sound's Orca whales from PCB poisoning with a friend as if I were discussing a recipe. I was numb. I could not feel anything. I feared that I was losing my humanity.

For years, I had dreamed of spending a week with the wind, water, and a thousand years of old growth in Canada's Great Bear Rainforest. Perhaps now was a good time to take a break. The wilderness had always had a way of restoring my soul. Still, I wondered if I was too far gone.

Once inside Cornwall Inlet, surrounded by steep walls of glacier-carved granite, we were cut off from the outside world for at least twenty-four hours—another two tide cycles. In the last moments of radio communication, to which we could only listen, we heard the terrible news uttered by two boats passing outside the entrance to the inlet and unaware of our presence. It was September 11, 2001. The World Trade Center towers had just fallen and the Pentagon was on fire. No planes were flying anywhere in North America.

I stood silently as one of my fellow passengers relayed the message from the radio. At first I was indignant. How dare the outside world invade my peace out here in the wilderness? I pushed aside the bad news and went on about my business of scanning the shore for signs of big mammals. I struggled to maintain the bliss of denial, while something heavy held tight in the back of my mind. At the time, I could not understand the magnitude of this act of violence. But slowly, in imperceptible moments, the horror of this deed took shape.

Once anchored within the snug security of wilderness, we planned a walk to look for bears. I donned a yellow life jacket, pulled on my tall, green hip boots and boarded the rubber-hulled Zodiac with the others. A light rain descended over us like a shroud. We were slow to discuss the tragedy. We were strangers and it didn't seem appropriate.

Once on shore, we walked upstream through high water and tall bushes of salal, huckleberry, and salmonberry. I struggled against my hip boots and layers of clothing that encased me like a suit of armor. I hid my preoccupation with world events in the silence of the forest and of the group as we searched for signs of bears. When we reached a shallow falls in the river, we found a log to sit on and wait, watching for bears that might come to the stream to fish for salmon.

In a deep drizzle, we sat in silence. The outside world invaded my thoughts and made it difficult to remember I was in a pristine rain forest. Images of Pearl Harbor, of WW II, of Hiroshima buzzed around me like the no-see-ums biting my face and hands with a force that belied their small size. No bears fished, the eagles had flown away, and I watched the salmon spend the last of their life energy to give birth to the next generation. Was this the beginning of

WW III? How many lives were lost? I had never felt more separate from the natural world.

Of all the questions that ran through my mind, I did not ask "why did this happen?" I thought of Ed, the seventy-year-old Heiltsuk elder from Bella Bella along on the trip. At age seven, he had been taken from his family by missionaries and placed in a residential school in Alert Bay. He was not permitted to speak his language or practice his culture. With long deep breaths, I contemplated the ancient power struggles around the world. I remembered the clear-cuts we'd flown over, vast valleys raped and scoured to the dark soil, the remaining desolation reminiscent of the holocaust. I began to understand the death of a spirit from deep despair and the loss of human dignity that could lead to this desperate act of suicide and murder. I remembered a saying I'd once heard, "Until all are free, none are free." One tear spilled down my cheek as a chill crept into my body.

That evening, as we squeezed around the heavy cedar table in the dimly lit cabin for dinner, we broke our silence and tested the water. "My daughter was supposed to fly home from Montana today," said Chuck, the leader of the trip, as he stared distantly into his plate, stroking his full gray beard. "I hope she made it okay." I had known this man only two days, but in that time I had sensed his deep devotion to his family. Another man reached over and placed a large hand on Chuck's shoulder as we continued passing the fresh salmon, new potatoes, and Caesar salad around the table in silence, each searching our minds for family or friends who might have been traveling.

"I can only imagine what those people in New York must be going through," someone added.

"How many people do you think...?" I asked, my voice trailing off as I realized I did not really want to know. At this time we had no idea that passenger planes had been hijacked. We knew nothing of the heroism shown by passengers of those ill-fated flights or of the last phone calls home from the World Trade Center. We knew nothing of the many police and firefighters lost as they tried to save lives. Yet, even without the images and rhetoric of the modern media, we began to understand the magnitude of the tragedy.

That night, I woke in the blackness of the wilderness and again the no-see-ums of worry swarmed around me. How many more innocent lives would be lost? What would this act of violence mean for all life on our planet?

The next morning, gathered around the breakfast table, we talked again—the boundaries of strangers melting away. "How did everyone sleep?" asked Eric, showing the customary concern of a captain for his guests as he stepped down into the cabin and took his seat beside Ed and Chuck.

"I woke up and couldn't get back to sleep," Chuck admitted first. "I just couldn't stop thinking about the people in New York." I glanced around the table at my fellow passengers to see heads nodding in agreement. "It's like there's a disturbance in the force. Remember *Star Wars*?"

"Yes," I said, realizing I had a physical sense of the world's collective shock growing and rolling toward us like a huge tidal wave. It was like something in the air around us had changed, like the very density of the molecules had shifted as the consistency of clean water changes after an oil spill. A friend, who used to guide float trips through the Grand Canyon, once told me, "during epic events, even though we were out in the wilderness, we could really feel something tactile," rubbing her fingers together as if touching a fine piece of fabric.

As breakfast was served, Eric asked Ed, the Heiltsuk elder, for his traditional blessing. With hands, gnarled from years of arthritis, folded together, Ed began his blessing in the words of his ancestors. As he spoke, the ancient syllables melded together in words I could not understand, until I heard him say "Boostons," the word he had told us meant "Americans." As he continued his blessing for the American people, he began to weep. He paused, "I pray for the suffering people. I'm so sad." We sat in silence, witnesses in the wilderness to a tragedy a world away.

Later that morning news of world events finally reached us through a group of anthropologists from several of the First Nation tribes in the area. They had come to Cornwall Inlet to study an ancient longhouse site on the Gitga'at Nation's land. "You guys hear what happened?" called the captain of the other boat as they motored slowly toward the Ocean Light. Eric nodded. "They used four passenger planes…" I heard the captain add as my attention shifted to the small groups of conversations going on around me, each telling of a new horror. I felt a wave of nausea and tightness in my throat. I struggled not to gag. Finding a quiet spot on deck, I stared into the water, while a new wave of shock and disbelief swallowed me whole.

As I struggled in the emotional quicksand, I noticed a plain, brown, finchlike bird sitting beside me. "Hi birdie," I said quietly. He responded with a few hops toward me, then paused and gazed in my direction. Cocking his head first one way and then the other, he considered me carefully with each shiny, black eye, as if to ponder my mood. I sat motionless as he came to his conclusions. His curiosity satisfied, he hopped around the deck investigating each tiny speck of debris or insect. I marveled at the fearlessness of this little bird, and began to watch intently as he visited first one and then another of us. The unusual behavior of this small bird and his seeming oblivion to the current struggles in the human world were a welcomed distraction for me. I smiled at the joy of surprise as each of my fellow passengers discovered our tiny visitor. A messenger from the gods, I thought, remember life.

After lunch, we headed ashore again to look for bears. We had seen two bears walking along the beach earlier in the day and were hopeful of a close encounter. With the thought of seeing more wildlife, my mood brightened. I began to absorb the magnificence of my surroundings. Tall mountain peaks dressed in a thin veil of morning mist stood in a semicircle at the head of the inlet, while tall cedars dripping with pale green lichen guarded the mouth of East Creek. There was not a better place to be as the world fell apart.

Once on the beach, we planned to make plaster casts of several wolf tracks we'd seen the day before. As I walked to the area where we'd sighted the tracks, a small bird whizzed by and landed a few feet ahead of me. The strangeness of the bird's behavior caught me by surprise before I realized it was the same small brown bird from the boat. "We should name him Imutu," someone suggested. "It's the Heiltsuk word for 'shadow.'" We continued searching for tracks on the beach as Imutu hopped along behind searching for bugs in our wake. I laughed at the ingenuity of my small companion.

As I bent over a wolf track imprinted in the dark mud of the beach, I imagined a large gray wolf running with its pack along the beach at low tide, its weight pressing its large paws deep into sandy mud. Was the pack running toward the river to fish for salmon? Did they stop to sing their haunting songs to the trees and the mountains? I examined the print and stooped to remove debris. Then I knelt down, dug my fingers into the dirt, and began to build a wall around the track. Images of childhood mud pies came to me. A smile swept over my face as I breathed deep the musky scent of commingled earth and sea. I sunk my fingers into the mud, kneading the soil like a loaf of bread, grabbing and letting go as the joy of creation from the earth jumped from the mud to my fingers. I turned my head to see Imutu hopping among the sparse stands of beach grass collecting bugs. The earth was still here; life continued.

As we waited for our plaster tracks to set, I wandered the beach looking for other tracks and played with Imutu when he flitted my way. I tried to convince myself, falling back on my years of scientific training, that he was just hanging around us because we were stirring up insects for his next meal. Yet, I sensed something deeper, a connection between species. I believed he was befriending us in our time of need, as a beloved cat or dog offers companionship during times of grief. I welcomed his cheerful company.

Later that evening, when we visited the longhouse where the anthropologists were studying, to share their fire and to listen to ancient legends, I would learn that Imutu had visited them as well. "A messenger, eh," one anthropologist from Haida Gwaii remarked without the self-consciousness of a traditional western scientist. My jaw dropped and I stood stunned by the coincidence of his observation.

After our plaster tracks had hardened, we continued our walk upstream, with Imutu hopping along behind until we crossed the river. Wearing our tall hip boots, we walked through the thigh-high water. Splashing through the water was much easier than stepping over hip-high bushes, and I giggled as my legs floated with every step. We soon reached the area where we'd waited for bears the day before and crossed the shallow river to a low island covered by tiny round pebbles and boulders worn smooth by the water's constant flow. As I found a comfortable seat, I recognized several deep holes in the stream, where salmon hid under fallen logs. Nearby, I heard the swishing of powerful tails of the large male salmon fighting over the perfect spot to spawn in the river. We waited and waited for bears.

Then, just as we were preparing to leave, a large black bear appeared at the edge of the stream. He walked along the very log we'd been sitting on the day before. The bear's shiny black coat reflected sparks of sunlight as he placed one foot in front of the other sideways like a gymnast on the balance beam. He paused periodically to gaze into the water, staring at the multitude of fish below him as if to calculate the ease of catching a meal. He dropped down from the log and continued in our direction. We stood silent, as motionless as standing stones.

But the bear looked directly at us, as if considering us in his wild mind. Then he sullenly turned toward the opposite shore since we had already claimed the prime fishing spot on the river. The bear seemed to turn away not so much because we were human but because there were more of us. Bears give way to dominance.

Moments later he crashed through the water throwing spray high into the air in pursuit of a salmon dinner. With one swift, fluid motion he bent over and plucked a flailing fish from the stream. Then he turned in our direction and paused, making eye contact seemingly to show us with bashful bear pride "look what I've got"—as if he felt he needed to prove himself to us, like a god revealing his uncertainty to his worshippers. I laughed out loud at his statement. Held in the consciousness of the wild and considered an equal, as if we had a place to share on the river, I felt less alone in my place as a human.

I looked around at the mountains towering over the stream. They stood as sentinels for eons, joined by thousand-year-old cedars and hemlocks. The salmon have followed an ancient call to return to this river, nourishing the birds, the bears, the trees. Life here continued on as it had for an eternity. Or did it?

As the afternoon grew older, I had managed to lose myself in the flow of life in this forest. Until the shadows lengthened and it was time to return to the Ocean Light—our tiny civilization in the middle of wilderness—I had forgotten the density of shock, lingering like the uneasy feeling before a storm or the thrill in the air between summer and fall.

Reluctantly, we had turned downstream to leave the bear in peace with his meal when we noticed a great blue heron balancing on a boulder at the edge of the island. He sat motionless, his long, thin neck curled like a snake under his chin, while his yellow eyes looked between the worlds of air and water. I quietly grabbed my camera from its bag and snapped a few photos of the heron before he flew away. Then we stepped slowly toward the heron and stopped, each prepared to capture on film or in memory, his moment of flight. The heron, however, remained undisturbed. We continued, inching closer. I struggled to move quietly in my plastic armor as I carefully placed each step against crunching gravel. We were within twenty feet. I raised my camera and held my breath as I prepared to capture his flight. But still the heron remained undisturbed.

"I've never been this close to a heron," Eric whispered. I would learn that the great blue heron had been the favorite bird of Eric's close friend, who had been killed in an accident. At his funeral, as friends scattered his ashes, a great blue heron circled overhead.

I let my camera fall and dangle around my neck. Then, the slow wrinkle of a question formed on my face as I paused to consider the growing list of unusually attentive behavior in the animals around me. I thought of Imutu offering friendship aboard the boat and on the beach and the acknowledgment from the bear. My heart beat in slow rhythm with my breath. I looked at the great blue heron, standing on the rock, unafraid. A jolt of recognition leapt in my chest and I swallowed hard. I wondered if the animals sensed the shock as we did, as if this tragedy resonated through the earth like an earthquake. Then, when the heron had our undivided attention and I met his bright yellow eye, I heard his voice in my heart. We know what happened to your world. We are sorry.

Silently, I thanked the heron as he lifted his pterodactyl wings and glided downstream. For a moment, we stood and looked at each other. Eric smiled, bowed his head, and walked downstream. Within two steps Chuck was by my side smiling. "I really needed this today," he said as he put his arm around me. "I was really hurting."

The grief we felt over the events of 9/11 and the ensuing U.S. retaliation would not pass quickly. Yet, as I remember my time in the Great Bear Rainforest, I feel a sense of renewal, a sense of peace somewhere in the world. I had always considered the importance of the forest in terms of its role as home to a vast array of birds, bears and wolves, and ancient trees, and for its function as lungs of the earth, sustaining physical life. In Cornwall Inlet, I understood the value of the wilderness as "Mother," as giver and sustainer of spirit, on the day the earth saved me.

Where the Mountains Meet

Lauri Dane

I STAND ON UNEVEN GROUND. Sticks jut out from the mud floor beneath my feet. There's water to my left, and a potential fall down a tangle of sharpened sticks is on the right. Streams spill into swampy ponds. I squat to sit on a birch branch, settling ever so softly. This is not a comfortable place to rest. Yet most days, I return. For it is here that I discovered place, a place in nature. Or, perhaps, rediscovered place. As with many children, who are more at home in the world than adults, when I was nine I knew place without understanding place. When I was nine, my place was the woods.

That was the year that my friend Lisa wanted to run away, and I volunteered to accompany her. "I'm going to run away," I told my mom. She made me a lunch of peanut butter and jelly. I folded a red bandana around the sandwiches and tied the sack to the end of a long stick, which I propped on my shoulder. "See you later, Mum." She knew where I was going. It was where I went every day.

Even in the early morning, the air was hazy, hot, humid—the three H's of Pittsburgh—and I was warm in a Snoopy Joe-

96

Cool T-shirt and jeans. I cut into the woods that were across the street, the woods that connected my house to Lisa's house, then spread out to the Nature Center. It was late summer and I felt alive going into the woods; it smelled like dirt. A buzz saw cut through the call of birds. My path was one along a loop of trails— these trails that were motocross for suburban kids on banana-seat bikes. I pulled leaves off a low tree and climbed onto a moss-covered boulder that presided over the foyer of the woods. "EEE-oo-Wee," I called for Lisa to hear. I crumbled the leaves in my palm; they smelled of popcorn.

This spot, this boulder top, was a tiny world to its own. Lichen crusted a paint of pale green that curled and chipped with age. Woody sprouts grew from the moss. Each strand of moss looked like a tree from a Dr. Seuss book. I pressed my hand into the moss to feel its spring. Looking under rocks was a favorite pastime of mine, so I checked under a flat rock to see the goods. Snails. I picked one up, and with small circles its antennae probed the air. There's so much in so little.

Lisa came running onto the trail. I jumped off the rock, and we ran as if we were being chased. We headed for the Nature Center, which was a small preserve in the woods. On Arbor Day, the center jumped. Families came for face painting, kids hammered out their names onto leather tags, and scouts handed out pine seedlings in plastic bags. There was music and bubbles in the air. But today, and most days, we were the only visitors.

We ran until we reached the creek at the Nature Center. I stashed my sack under an oak—some of western Pennsylvania's largest oak trees live here—and sat next to the water. Lisa's dark blue eyes cried the tears of an oldest daughter burdened with the care of younger siblings and wounded by the temper of an unhappy man. But here in the hollow, where the crayfish hid, she, too, found a respite.

Time passed and we returned home. But having that need for place, that need for a refuge, remained. Later that summer, I rode my bike on the trails and hit something that flipped me over the handlebars of my red, white, and blue Schwinn. The wind was knocked out of me. My chest heaved. I was puzzled. I knew all the bumps and grinds of these trails. What did I hit?

Sticking out from the dirt was a stake tied with orange flagging tape. Within weeks, the bulldozers arrived. Lisa and I sabotaged the heavy equipment, but filling the cockpit with rocks and dirt did not stop the Barelli's from moving in, then the Duffy's, then the Russo's.

For years, I lost the woods. And even after I became interested in hiking, I was removed. Even when I lived in the mountains, I was removed. There was a boundary between the woods and myself. The boundary was the car.

My boyfriend and I packed our cars. Graduate school, for me, was over. After three years in the city, I longed to return to New England. I missed hearing the peepers; I missed kicking stones on dirt roads; I missed seeing boys in pickups and girls wearing flannel. We drove to Vermont, then drove around Vermont until we found the town we wished to call home. The real estate market was tight, and we rented the only place we found in our price range: cheap.

Days after we moved in, Dave said to me, "You're going to flip when you see what's out there." He led me down our dirt road. At the end of the road, woods began. It neared the end of

October, and the air was still and cool. Near a cabin with a rotting porch and duct tape on the window, we dipped into the woods, which were bright with the yellow of birch leaves and the red of young maple trees. I followed Dave over a small creek, a runoff from a small rise to the right. We cut left into a spruce forest, an older forest with a few old, thick maple trees. Clover covered the forest floor. I saw water through the trees, and we walked down a steep incline. I was awed.

I stood on a beaver dam. To the left was a large pond that was old enough that no dead trees stood in the water—there was just the still reflection of tall pines in the water. Two beaver lodges were built into the water. One backed up into a swampy area; the other was protected by pines. To the right, to the south, a valley extended. This valley view rolled out for miles with marshes and ponds. An evergreen forest edged this open space. Three mountains framed the backdrop, lovely, rounded mountains. All I saw is wild—no roads, no houses, and no evidence of people.

Three years pass, and I still feel awe each time I scramble down the slope, step onto the beaver dam, and see this scene. This sense of awe gave us the word nature—nature is derived from the Latin word natura, which means birth, constitution, or the order of things. Birth. Rebirth. Each day, I am reborn. I would have refrained from admitting something so cliché until I learned the word's origin. This rebirth is ritual, not only my ritual, but also anyone and everyone who fell silent from beauty, anyone and everyone who lost themselves and their drama for a minute, and just was.

My visits are now ritual. At the entrance to the woods, at the end of the road, a falcon that is perched on a branch watches as I step into the woods. As if stepping into another world, and aided by this gatekeeper of the wild, my soul hushes. The tension in my face fades, my eyes relax. Breathe. I slow my breathing. It is a hot August morning, and it smells of dirt. I feel warm and full of heart. The trees are young and deciduous, so light spills in and ferns blanket the floor and reach high—tall, thigh-high ferns. I fan my hand over the tips, and the ferns respond with sway. The sun rises above my three peaks, a beautiful welcome to each day, and the sky ahead of me is cast in the colors of morning. I step in moose tracks hardened by the late summer dry spell. I saw my first moose in the wild here, in these woods. It was also here, in these woods, that I first saw a beaver, a great blue heron, an otter, an owl, and a snowshoe hare in the wild.

It is on the dam this hot August morning that I hear a whirl, a deep whirl. I turn and see a hummingbird. What joy—a hummingbird out of the confines of cultivation. So common in the yard, so extraordinary in the wild. The hummingbird approaches different flowering plants until she finds her food choice: the jewel weed. I had pulled this plant from my yard, disregarded it as an invasive when it passed the border of my yard, even though I know that in the wild, this plant is a tonic to the feathery stinging nettle (and with nature's harmony, the two plants grow as neighbors). This weed feeds the hummingbird. This weed heals my wounds. I am stuck in the world so wrought with the human perspective that it takes several prods, several clues left by nature, for me to see any other perspective. Now I will assign a different value on this plant, for this plant attracts a bird we revere as an epitome of beauty, a bird whose iridescence captures us so much that we name it after our most prized possession—jewels. This red-throated beauty draws nectar from the fluted bloom.

This is wild I have never known. This wild brews with life when nobody watches, and nobody watches regularly. During the three years I have explored this area, I have seen two people. People live on the edge of these woods, but few venture in. So, this land is my intimate, and the bond grows. Knowing place within nature is like knowing a lover. In the beginning of exploration, I see the most prominent features, the curves of the landscape. Soon I identify the trees and pick up animal signs. Then I recognize the animals' patterns of movement, identify their motivations. Then I notice areas of growth, areas in which certain beauty thrives. With some years, I anticipate seasonal changes, life stages, and moods. I know when a mushroom will pop up, where the trillium will grow, what time of year to look for the iris in the swamp. It's like a walking memory, and each stroll adds one more nuance.

Knowing something intimately helps me better understand the world around me. I have learned the why and the how of these woods; I see layers of meaning that can be used to decipher other landscapes. Understanding expands my comfort zone. Until I lived here, I was afraid to venture off trail. But that is where discovery begins. And like a spiral, the path of awareness circles outward.

This spiral begins with beaver; my spiral begins with the beaver—the only animal besides man that can transform a landscape. And here, at the base of these mountains, I discovered transformation on a grand scale—at the base of the mountains there are at least twenty beaver ponds in various stages of development. Newly dammed ponds have hillsides marked by the lethal leftovers of freshly harvested beech trees—sharpened stakes that could drive through a vampire's heart. Dams that were recently vacated become swamps striped with watery channels. Dens abandoned long ago have turned to marsh, and remain lovely with tall grasses, young birch and beech, baby pines, cattails, and a remnant pond at the epicenter. So, this rodent—a rodent—creates an ecosystem.

This amazes me. The beaver builds its homestead, and this homestead becomes a gathering point for many species, a gathering point that breathes life into other mammals, birds, insects, and flora. And me.

Wild animals come for food; I come for beauty and the beaver. There are five who live in the big pond, four adults and one young gun. The best time to see them is at dusk, for they are nocturnal and begin their work with the sunset. Sometimes all five will pop up as I watch. They are aware of my presence, and they swim with an eye on me. It is the eldest male that urges me to leave with a slap of his tail. I do not wait long to walk away after this warning. I am the visitor in their world.

But I do return regularly, and one morning in August, I arrive to Venus's glow in the dawn sky. A cap of cloud hangs on the mountains. The moon has yet to fade, for this was a late rising moon—it was still out of view when Dave and I walked the dog last night. Though it was dark, we walked to the pond; I was excited to check out the night sky because the Perseid meteor shower heats up this time of year. As we watched meteors slice the sky, we saw the loveliest of surprises—aurora borealis. Blackness of sky boomed with light flashes, which then raised like distortion off a hot fire. People stand across from one another at a bonfire and see distortion of space; I peered across a universe and wondered who looked back, wondered who answered my request for a wild space in my midst.

Dawn warms up to a lovely morning. I sit on a log and watch the clouds move. The sun behind the clouds casts a rose gold to the morning. A breeze blows, a warm breeze. Trees sway, leaves shimmer, grasses flow. Wind moves across the water so easily. If only I could carry with me this grace. This morning, I stepped over a moose track. Its hoof had sunk into the mud about three inches, and a spider cast its web across the moose print. Beautiful. This folding together of hands, this interlocking of fingers, this peaceful combination honors what is unique, what is nature.

The next morning is still. I take off my shirt to stretch in the warm, moist heat. I feel my blood pulse. It is a quiet world at the pond, and by 7:00 A.M. most of the animals have retreated to the shade. A hummingbird hums in, drinks from its jewelweed, and flies into the heart of the swamp alder and rests on a branch. Never have I seen a hummingbird rest. Most mornings, the dog stands by my side watching the buzz of morning activity. This morning, he lays in the shade beneath a pine tree with his tongue hanging out of his mouth and into the dirt. The air is quiet, few birds call. Brush strokes of clouds pass the sun and provide moments of relief. Black-eyed Susans droop in the heat. The only creatures out in full throttle are the bugs. The surface of the pond looks as if rain falls. *Ping. Ping. Ping.* Bugs land on the surface, their landing circles ever-widening. Bubbles rise from the muck at the bottom of the pond. I have no idea what lurks under the muck. I poke the muck with a stick, feel resistance as if I touched something, then retract my stick. Let it be. Who lives and what happens beneath the surface is a mystery to me. This is okay.

There is always mystery in the wilderness. I can learn the myths and the histories; I can learn the behaviors of the animals; I can connect with my landscape and feel it as my place, but she is wild and moves on her own, tolerates me, but does not welcome me. When a heron flies above and sees me, its long sail between wing flaps stops short and the bird rises with a jerk, as if yanked by a string from the heavens. The beaver slaps his tail at me. The moose turn and walk away—like our first encounter one autumn morning when Dave and I were walking the dog. We heard a loud snap. The dog froze and pointed. A loud lumbering *crash-crash-crash* followed, and the dog took off. We looked at each other—only a large animal would make that sound. Fast and as stealthily as we were able, we ducked under trees and followed the dog. We approached the edge of a pine grove that stands next to a boggy section between two ponds, and there a moose stood in the water. The steam of early morning rose from the bog, and her heat produced steam. She looked around, as if scanning for potential trouble. I felt guilty as I watched her, but I did not turn away until she retreated. With the steam and her size and her very wildness and the mountains in the background, it was a scene that burns into the brain. We were moments from our house, and the world was wild.

We felt the need to name our way around. "From thence on, this shall be called Moose Trail." We have since named Lollipop Loop, Lollipop Handle, Owl Corner, Bright Hill, Birdbox Pond, Christmas Tree Meadow, Upper Pond, Mystery Pond I, Mystery Pond II, Bunny Hollow, Grassy Meadow, Grassy Meadow Pond, Magic Trails, Tall Pine Alley, Bird Hill, Crystal Trail, and the BPs. On my thirty-second birthday, three weeks after we got engaged, Dave surprised me with Lauri's Trail, which he had built. Why do we want to name? If a place remains unnamed, does it remain too separated, too wild? Do we hope to tame our surroundings—is this our nature, just as the beaver longs to dam his surroundings? Or do we wish to identify and quantify our surroundings just so they make sense?

So many lovely flowers bloom at the pond: pink and fuzzy blooms look like a pretty girl's angora sweater, pale purple flowers resemble old-fashioned roses; there's a yellow version of echinacea; white flowers smell of baby's breath, smoky pink flowers weave the pattern of Queen Anne's lace, asterlike flowerets are cast in yellow and purple; I see bright orange cups, yellow mustardlike plants, violet-colored tendrils, white bells with burgundy veins. I know no names—does this make these beauties any less lovely, any less real?

Dampness wipes out the crispness of the next morning, wipes out the crispness of my perception. The day rises above the mountain in a smoke screen of gray and mist. Fog clings to the treetops and skates across the water. It rained last night, so the leafy greens look slick. Time and sun burn off this haziness, this dreaminess of dawn. Light illuminates droplets of water caught in the spider webs. The weaves of web glow like a fluorescent light in the dark. There are about fifty webs within my sight—some one hundred feet away and some thirty feet high in dead trees. Never did I realize how many spiders were spinning their stuff. I crouch down and look into the droplets that line the strands of one web, and watch the world reflect back to me. The web pulses in the air as a whole, yet each filament moves independently with its own rhythm. This web catches the wind and catches the sun and catches me. It is more beautiful than a jewel. To appreciate this is to appreciate God. How lucky I am to see this, to know this.

My family deems me peculiar. To find life in life rather than possessions, to seek the world in the world rather than a high-priced store—this is, to them, quite queer. My interest in the woods is seen as frivolous. What they do not know is that my interest in the woods is all there is. My interest in the woods is religious. God speaks to me in nature, not in holy texts. When I see the mountains in the morning, I know God. Do we all have a landscape—a landscape that helps us know God? The woods are God; a leaf is God; God is the fog the obscures the mountain. We have churches to tell of God, but nature shows God, raw and perfect.

The next day, I head out early. Dawn is blue. Not the blue of a hot summer sky, not the blue of ocean water, but the blue of change, the blue of a different air. Cool wind blows through the trees. I inhale—the brightness of summer's scent has aged. The ever-so-lovely scent of rotting ferns has arrived. It is a heady smell, like frankincense and myrrh. Though official fall is but a month away, she is in the air. In the woods, the flowers have turned to seed. Trilliums hang long, fleshy red pods of seed. Bunchberry's white flower transforms into a cluster of red seeds. Yellow bells produce seeds of blue, a blue I have never seen in the woods—it's the blue of night buffed with the shine of pearl. Soon, the seeds will drop, then leaves will drop and wrap the seeds in their cold weather blanket.

A hummingbird announces herself; she is tiny and strong, delicate and hardy. This may be the last time I see the hummingbird in the wild for this year. She leaves for the tropics soon; she will fly thousands of miles. I leave for the city soon; I will drive hundreds of miles. I am going to be married, married far from this landscape. How I wish I could carry with me not only what I see, but what I feel when I stand surrounded by mountains and trees and water and life.

Today, my shirt clings from humidity, yet the wind blows in autumn air. The eastern sky is blue; ominous grays drive in from the west. The last summer flowers bloom next to a maple that drops fall's red leaves. Transition time.

We fall into autumn as a married couple, married on the Harvest Moon. The months pass quickly as my husband and I walk in the woods—this walking in the woods is the soul of our love. It seems too soon, but it's time to leave again. I feel apprehensive to leave my landscape, but we have moved into winter, to Christmastime, and this means going to our hometown. When I visit the city, it is not the city of my childhood. It is not buildings and concrete that I deem depressing; it is the lack of character that is becoming the city's character that disheartens me. The world outside of my world moves ever faster in a direction away from the wild of life, away from unpredictability of life.

At least we will see our family. We plan to meet my dad at the latest hot spot, a riverfront complex built at the site of the former steel mills. With shops and theaters and restaurants, what a wonderful place is this place, I was told. What a wonderful revitalization of a dead space, I think.

The snow falls as my husband and I drive the streets of the city. We cross a bridge and see a crowded parking lot that spreads far out, far away from the main attraction. We pass aisles and aisles of cars. As we get closer, we see the attraction is a town center; in the middle of this vast lot is an intersection of streets around a town green. But this town is not real: this is a mall of a different design, a mall in small-town clothing. The businesses lined by electric, gas-lit-style street lamps are chain stores. Restaurant chains garner street corner status. Plopped on the town green is a gazebo-shaped Starbucks.

It is two days before Christmas. The streets are busy with shoppers walking with their full shopping bags. The snow still falls. My heart falls still.

Perhaps I could feel encouraged that the latest commercial success is conceived around the idea of a town green; perhaps this means people long to experience the small town. But I do not; I feel defeat.

The longer this trend continues, the more difficult it will be to break its chains. This chaining of America binds us to uniformity. We expect the expected. If surroundings grow more and more alike, how can sense of place survive? We connect to place when we experience the uniqueness of that place. If we lose this, if we lose this sense of place, we lose the sense of caring about a space. When everything is the same, nothing matters. And what a loss to us—as we become nature illiterates, will we find a landscape that helps us to feel God?

We return to our home in Vermont on New Year's Eve. The snow falls as my husband and I wind down our dirt road. We live at the southern end of a valley. A river flows north through the valley heart, and this valley is framed by two mountain chains, which meet in a V in our space. It is here, where the mountains meet, that we live the grace of place. And it is now, during winter, when this world of the woods expands. While many pull in, tuck into their homes in this dead of winter, the lucky folks discover the life of winter.

On New Year's Day, my husband and I decide to ice skate. We gather snow shovels, skates, and buckets for sitting and head for the pond. Ice frosts the mountaintops in the background. Pines line our road, and the branches brush the ground with the weight of snow. In the summer, our road is a lovely country lane with grass growing in the center. In the winter, even the plowman ends up in the ditch. Sweet and green in the summer, impossible and impassable in the winter. But there is no lack of traffic; animal tracks are everywhere. The dog is manic; he runs with his nose to the ground following the paths of prints. Rabbits are busy around here; there are visible rabbit roads and crossroads that go undetected in the summer. Fox tracks lead to holes nestled in dead trees and hillsides. Along the spine of a downed tree, I spy a fisher's pad prints. It's magic to see the patterns of creatures that are rarely seen, the elusive animals of the kingdom. My eyes are full with the scene. We arrive at the pond and throw down our loads. The sun is high. Wisps of clouds pass near the sun and catch the prism reflection—moving, alive rainbows pass over me. The contrast of colors—a bluebird sky and the deep greens of pine and the white sparkle of snow and the rose tint of faraway deciduous trees—how this moves me, how this moves me each day. We work hard pushing heavy snow; I grunt and sweat drips down my belly.

Many hours later, we have a small rink. As we skate, the stage of sky is lit with a neon sunset; its orange and pink and gold reflect on the mountains. I think of my world of the past week, my world in the city, with the neon of fast food and the pallor of homogenization. The contrast between these two worlds, my two worlds, could not have been greater. The wild world provides us with mystery; the wild world challenges us. The homogenized world dulls us; the homogenized world skews us. When I live in one world, the other world seems unreal; like when I am depressed I can't imagine feeling happy, and when I'm happy I can't imagine feeling depressed. The world, the same world, can appear so different, be so different from day to day.

When I wake the next morning, the world is awash in softness. Last night's snow rounds the undulations in the land, and the ground appears warm and welcoming, like the arms of a mother. The sun has not yet risen atop the mountains. It is light without brightness, just a fade of grays, blues, and dusty whites that spread onto the landscape. The only vividness is the curled leaves of the beech tree, leaves of gold that hang on through the winter. Snow cover transforms the woods into one pathless path, which opens the door to the wild, to previously impassable places. I head into the woods with a peanut butter and jelly sandwich wrapped in a red bandana. I wander off-trail to follow what catches my whim. I know where I am going. It's where I go every day.

Fire Line

Jennifer DePrima

THE OTHER DAY while flipping through my planner looking for some long-lost phone number, I stumbled across a quote scribbled on a yellow Post-it. I had frequently heard people say, "What doesn't kill you makes you stronger," and thought it was a remarkably stupid saying: you can't get stronger if you're dead. Then I read this version—I have it attributed to Nietzsche, but I'm not convinced that's right either. I read "What does not destroy me makes me strong." That stuck. There are various forms of destruction. At twenty-six, I am starting to look at events in my life and wonder how I got through them, how they changed me, whether they have made me stronger or just afraid. At sixteen, I was afraid of moths and public confrontation. Now I fear immolation and becoming my mother.

One day I wake up feeling awful—upset stomach, headache, sore muscles, burning flesh—all the little symptoms of thousands of diseases. I call out from work and go back to bed. Two hours later I wake up well. I can't possibly go into work now; they will think I'm a hypochondriac or a liar. I grab my camera and head for the woods where I mountain bike. I can use a day off. I am tired all the time lately, pushing myself with grad school and work and new marriage and old friends and gym membership, yearning to make everything work, manufacture time; I wind up burning the candle at both ends, lying awake nights trying to organize it all.

There is a section of forest that captivates me every time I ride through it. I want to try to examine it more closely and recreate the mood of the place on film. I walk there, about five hundred yards from the Depot Road parking lot, a patch of forest filled with red pines. As I walk toward them I notice that the trees to the right of the fire road are significantly taller than the trees on the left. They are older, too, with thicker trunks and more branches. I raise my camera and compose the shot, trying to get both sides of the road into the frame to show how the trees rise and rise and rise, almost part of the sky, and then, across the path, reach higher. I haven't taken photos for a while; I doubt I will get the shot I want.

I keep walking down the fire road with the camera hanging around my neck. The wood to the left entrances me. Rows and rows of red pines, telephone-pole straight, fill the air with their scent and cover the forest floor with a soft layer of red-orange needles. They are all the same size, these trees. It is amazing. This place makes me think of California, though I have never been there. This is how I imagine redwoods look. I stand alone in the forest with sun in my eyes filtered down through the opening cut for the road.

I wonder why the trees are like this: all the same size and age, why so little else grows here, why it has such a strange uniformity. There are few other plants here. Ferns give the place a prehistoric feel. There are a few maple and oak saplings, but the tallest are only a foot or so taller than I am. I think I see some low-bush blueberry as well, but that's all. The pines seem to have been a monoculture for quite some time. As I continue down the jeep road, my eyes light on the sign at the trailhead. "Fire Line." How could I have missed the connection?

I stare and wonder what this place looked like before it burned. Some things were probably the same—the contours of the ground, the glacial rocks that rest serene among the trees. I wonder if the trees before were thicker, if there were different kinds, or if it was all red pines like it is now. Does the new growth mimic the old? I look around: I am aroused. The scent of the pine has triggered a memory of illicit high school sex, my back pressed against a tree trunk with smoldering skin exposed. Once I reached high school I was afraid to go hiking with my mother, worried that my face would color and give me away whenever we passed too close to the sites of my encounters. She must have known.

I keep walking along the edge of Fire Line. The jeep road forms the edge, dividing what burned from what did not. Further up, the trail forks and I bear to the left. Here the edge is less clearly delineated; there are trees of more varied heights and different plants along the forest floor. My inexperienced eye cannot discern whether this was part of the fire. Solomon's seal or false Solomon's seal reaches toward my leg. Without the flowers I don't know which. I look closer into the tops of the trees until I find the line where all the trees are same-sized red pines again. Fire Line. After about half an hour of close inspection, I realize that I can always find the line that separates the new growth from the unscarred part.

I can find the line where my scarring started. It is a May night; I am fourteen years old, in the back seat of some guy's Cadillac. Southern Comfort burns in my stomach and Dave's words burn in my ears—"I think I might very well be in love," he whispers, soft, so his friend who is driving won't hear. "Come on." I whimper and shake my head, turn my face away. Hot breath on my neck—I mouth the word "Stop" but don't know if he hears me and then my little white shorts are off. Searing pain and then he erupts.

I wonder how long after the fire this land lay bare. Did things begin to grow again at once, or did the burned patch gape up at the sky waiting for the ash to be carried away? Things must have begun to grow quickly—small plants, flowering plants, taking advantage of the sudden sunlight like the boys took advantage of my newly exposed sexuality. Did fire make the place vulnerable? Can places be vulnerable, or just the inhabitants? I imagine displaced birds and squirrels, creatures left with no safe place to nest. No—they would have time to escape the flames. I remember reading about a woodpecker that requires fire for survival. Something about the fire changes the tree so the bird can feed? I don't remember. I know other animals depend on the way fire clears away clutter from the forest floor. Deer will feed on the small plants that initiate the process of regrowth. Burnt-out roots and stumps start new hiding holes. I always notice tons of chipmunks here.

When I am in high school, my mother feels obligated to tell me how much different her childhood was from mine. I am an only child; she was the oldest of four. Boys in high school did not like her, she says. She was shy and too skinny. Boys liked Aunt Shirley. She was a hot ticket, my mother says, then gives me a disapproving look. I want to tell her that boys don't really like me; they just know I won't fight them. She thinks I do it on purpose and she is angry. She has to know I tell them no. I am certain that my name and number have been added to the graffiti on the bathroom walls where the boys huddle with their cigarettes between classes.

My mother does not see this; she is too busy watching for spontaneous combustion. Her father was an alcoholic. Nobody ever knew what spark would send him up. She tells me about coming down the stairs one night to find him standing in the living room holding one lit match. All the furniture was piled in the center of the room under the rug. "Whatcha doin', Pop?" she asked.

"Shhhh," he'd turned to her. "I'm looking for Hiawatha."

I am looking for something in these pines, some sign that they are stronger than their counterparts across the trail. Is the wood of the new trees somehow different? If I could look inside each tree, I could find its line. Where the fire passed through, it scorched the trees. But the trees keep adding rings; new cells enclose the charcoal, and the dark burn marks, the scars, stay invisible inside the trees.

I can keep my fire line invisible too, if I want to. I used to want that—to keep it hidden. I don't any more. I mark my growth from that line—I know I have become stronger. Strength is such a relative thing, so intangible. Can a place have strength? The soil is richer now—it has absorbed the nutrients from the ash, which will be put back into the new plants, my low-bush blueberry and Solomon's seal. I sit down on the ground and take my camera off over my head. I lean back against one of the post-fire trees and just breathe.

I imagine that I smell smoke, then decide I am hallucinating. I remember other smoke smells: toasting marshmallows at the Girl Scout camp I hated, the thick patchouli incense I burned in my room to cover up the scent of the cigarettes I stole from my grandmother, the angry gasoline odor left after my grandfather ignited my uncle's truck. It was a glorious old truck, something from the 1940s that my Uncle Ray had pulled out of the junk-yard. He was going to restore it, and my mother was going to give it a hot-rod paint job. My grandfather got sick of looking at the truck and gave it a different kind of flame job, as if the smoke from this truck would obscure his visions of the truck he drove out of Dachau.

Other members of the family believe that the neighbors called the cops while my grandfather sat and watched it burn, a sacrifice to the great god Thunderbird, the god whose bottles littered our backyard. No one else's memory is too clear on this; they have all repressed it. I was six years old. I remember the truck.

I wonder if my grandfather's alcoholism made my mother stronger or destroyed her. Did it keep her so busy protecting everyone else that she has forgotten how to care for herself? She sat in the hospital waiting room crocheting afghans while cancer consumed my grandfather's throat as rapid as wildfire, in spite of the chemotherapy that blistered his innards. She is so busy staring at the site of the old conflagrations that she does not see that the wind has shifted—I am being engulfed from another direction. She never asked me what happened that May night or any of the nights afterward—nights I came home blazing with rage that my "no" was not enough. She never asks—she just condemns me. I am incensed. I want her to suffer for her assumptions, hope that guilt will tear at her like Prometheus's eagle.

There is a sudden flutter of wings rising up—I do not see the bird but I can hear. I imagine birds returning to the burned woods to build new nests like the mythical phoenix; new life rising from the ash.

Is the core of Fire Line the same, with only surface changes? Or has the change in the trees, plants, and inhabitants of the place made it a different place altogether, somewhere that it was not before the fire? Does my surface remain the same while my center has been tempered? I don't think so—the changes to my core are visible. Fire leaves an indelible mark. One can see the scars, the places licked by flames.

What seems like a devastating fire can clear away detritus and leave a richer base for growth. It is a weeding out, a preparation for what comes next. Fire Line and I. We have been tempered. We were not destroyed.

The Garden of Live Flowers

April Heaney

Come, hearken then, ere voice of dread,
With bitter tidings laden,
Shall summon to unwelcome bed
A melancholy maiden!
We are but older children, dear,
Who fret to find our bedtime near.
—Lewis Carroll, *Through the Looking Glass*

WHEN MY FAMILY MOVED to Casper, Wyoming, from Chicago in 1980, I was five years old. My parents drove slowly through the valleys, talking about deer as if they were field spirits that could be spotted only with concentration. I peered through the car window and tried to quiet my thoughts, believing the deer might be fooled by the silence into leaving their hiding places. If a tentative snout appeared from the yellow grass, I felt powerful, able to evoke deer from the light Wyoming air.

From our living room window, we could see Casper Mountain stretching to the south of town, a snaky, bluish hill. After years of admiring the view, my mother suggested we take a day trip to explore the trails. The Saturday morning was cold, and I lagged behind my parents and older sister, picking my way across the rocky path and watching for poison ivy. Always seeking an excuse to feel left out, I moped, determined that I would not enjoy myself. In late morning I looked up to see a doe standing ten feet from me. With ears pricked, she appeared ready to flee at the next sound. All self-pity vanished and I held myself still, pressing my arms to my sides and marveling at her nearness.

Many minutes passed while we stared at each other. I began to will for the wariness in her eyes to disappear. You can trust me, I thought, trying to telepathically communicate my benevolence to the doe. One step, I thought, one step toward me and I will understand the sign, know that you hear me. My eyes actually teared with the intensity of my desire for a connection; her next move could confirm every mystical power I believed I possessed— make me better than anyone else on earth. An awkward and self-conscious eight year old, I wanted desperately to feel unique, and I remember how the sun shone against the backs of the trees, causing the woods to glow with supernatural possibilities.

Faces around the table reflect a variety of feelings: boredom, confusion, eagerness, feigned interest. My college English theory class is discussing Lewis Carroll's Through the Looking Glass, and we pore over the scene where Alice wanders into the wood where things have no names and meets a fawn. "The wood has obscured their identities," our professor recaps, "and the two walk through the trees as companions, Alice's arms around the fawn's neck. What does this tell us?" The conversation buzzes of "signifieds" and "signifiers," how language inevitably constructs our identities and defines the boundaries of our lives. I sit mute for once, overcome by a childhood memory of standing alone on Casper Mountain, ready to be transformed by the trust of a wild doe. I feel empathy for Alice, deflated after the fawn recognizes her and flees outside the wood. She, like me, must have experienced a brief inner calm, a sensation of almost transcending the laws of humanity. When the moment ended, she must have felt reality rush back with a sprinkling of dull mortality.

In my mid-twenties, I have begun to think about death with morbid frequency. These thoughts seem absurd to me, but they are persistent. When I look in the mirror, I see little wrinkles around my eyes and mouth that don't go away, even with a good night's rest and expensive lotions promising instant results. The first signs that time is irreversible are making their way into my life. As a child, I figured I would be married with children and a pension by age twenty-two. At twenty-six, I am dangerously close to thirty and no closer to figuring out who I am. A recent dream has left its colors on my mind for weeks: a dream of watching my family slip down a long tunnel to meet death waiting at the end. As my turn approached, I felt overpowering fear. I believe in God, I reminded myself. But if I really believed in God, I wouldn't be afraid, right? I woke up with dread tingling through my chest like a potent spiritual vinegar.

My boyfriend, a confirmed atheist, tries to put human mortality in greater perspective. He believes the world will be a better place when humanity reaches extinction, mostly because the natural world will be free from our harm. Animals are sacred, he says— but not in a religious way. "Maybe it's just that I feel sorry for them," he says, "living their lives always afraid; there are so many things that could kill them at any moment."

When I am close to a deer, it is this fear I respond to. My own niggling anxieties are dwarfed by the animal's constant, moment-to-moment need to be aware; its awareness of me makes otherwise muted aspects of me shine. I feel my secure place in the world, a maternal longing to calm—I feel a hint of the power I experienced as a child, conjuring deer from behind the window of our rundown Volkswagen Rabbit.

I have stroked the neck of a wild deer and fed her from my hand, and I can describe the feeling: the doe's lips are stiff and strong, brushing oats out of my palm with surprising aggressiveness. She does not seem to look me in the face. Her movements are quick, insistent, nervous, as if her muscles are pulled by invisible strings. She is steeped in wild, and I sense that she is willfully defying instinct and cannot be at peace. Her coat is matted, but her black eyes have the gloss of ripe plums. I touch her slender neck lightly and wish I could bring my adolescent self to meet this deer, to feel the life in her as tenuous and shimmering as a single strand of hair.

At the base of Casper Mountain, wild mule deer congregate in the road looking for handouts. They have been coming to this bend in Garden Creek Road since 1984 when Milo and Susan Anderson fed them processed corn feed from their nearby backyard. The winter of '84 was incredibly cold. I remember walking home from fourth grade with hands pressed over my face to keep my eyes from freezing shut with wind-induced tears. School was cancelled on a Tuesday because of the cold instead of snow—a rare and celebrated event. The Andersons felt sorry for the shivering deer that wandered through their property and fed the animals thirty pounds of corn every day.

The next fall, even though the extreme cold did not return, the deer did, hanging around the Anderson's property waiting for their meals. They were persistent. Soon, the surrounding residents noticed deer nibbling their gardens and trampling their fences and expensive landscaping. One Garden Creek resident shot his .410 shotgun over the deer's heads and hardly caused a stir. Within a few years, Garden Creek residents had claimed $8,400.00 in property damage to the Natrona County Commission. The Andersons, now the most unpopular couple on the block, reduced their supply of corn feed to five pounds a day and fed only the does. Still, the deer came.

When curious travelers stopped to photograph the small herds, they found the animals bold. Deer ventured close enough to be tempted with car food. Soon, the responsibility for feeding the deer passed from the Andersons to Casper residents and tourists. No one driving by the surreal sight of a dozen or more wild mule deer eating from the hands of children could resist stopping and offering whatever scraps were in the car.

Not surprisingly, wildlife experts warned against the feeding, explaining that deer are not as efficient as cows or sheep at digesting even low-quality forage, much less the Big Macs and Twinkies travelers offered. The deer's digestive tract can adapt to a new diet, but only very slowly. They can easily die of acidosis, a buildup of acid in the rumen if they overeat low-quality grain. If they lack enough microbes to digest large amounts of processed food, they will starve to death with full bellies. Besides causing malnutrition, feeding deer can hurt populations by allowing weaker animals to survive and breed. Despite these warnings, people refused to stop feeding the deer. One woman, angry at the city's attempts to curb the feedings, wrote to the editor of the Casper Star Tribune: "What other state has a sight such as this—none— because the people have crowded them out and killed them for their own selfish pleasure. Leave the deer alone! They belong to all of us, not just a few" (italics mine). Most of us were guilty of seeing the Garden Creek deer as our own private petting zoo.

The first deer I saw up close arrived at our apartment building slung over my father's shoulder when I was about nine. He had been on his first hunting trip, and while he managed to miss everything he aimed at, his companion offered the deer as a gift. I took one close look before my dad skinned his pseudo-trophy. Seeing the carcass stirred feelings of revulsion and fascination in my stomach. The deer was too ugly to be real with its dull, sticky coat and swollen tongue. A black scar ran along its muzzle like tiny beads of tar. I could not stop staring at its eye, the first lifeless eye I had ever seen. Open and entirely black, it looked glazed, a drop of syrup beginning to dry on the kitchen floor.

The first night the deer hung in our shed I had a nightmare that I jabbed a pointed stick into that eye, watching the black mass quiver and adhere to the stick. As hard as I tried, I could not remove the stake, and I felt a wash of fear. The following day I stayed far away from the shed where the skinned deer hung by its hind legs, white sinew visible from every corner of the backyard.

My father came home with packages of deer sausage and deer jerky, and I began to obsess over the idea of eternity. I decided to try and absorb the length of time one spends dead. One hundred thousand years, two hundred thousand, three hundred thousand... four? The sheer stamina of time pressed on me with unbearable weight. I lay in bed one night, rigid with the realization that I would die.

Some time after midnight I left my bed and crept downstairs to where my mom slept on the couch. Strands of blond hair hung limp against her forehead, and her open lips were dry. I watched her hands, folded over her stomach, to see if they moved with her breathing. When I saw they did not move, I believed that she had died. Tremendous sadness and guilt closed in. Somehow, my thoughts of death had killed her with their intensity. The hamburgers we had for dinner were a little pink: she had died of food poisoning. I imagined the awful finality of death hung around her in nightmarish proportions. When she opened her eyes, bleary with sleep, I started from where I crouched over her body, weeping. I returned to bed limp and ashamed, but with a lasting impression of the magnitude of death.

What I wonder is, would it be easier to fear death in the form of a mountain lion or hunter than in a gradual succumbing to amassing wrinkles? If I could creep into a deer's mind, would life snap into focus, revealing all of its colors and sounds and sensations in one amazing shutter click? Would I forget about eternity, about the complete obliteration of my self from the universe's memory? What kind of creature loves herself so much that she can't stomach the thought of ceasing to be? Death, I might realize with some relief, is always soon. Death is present. If I find a lanky girl before me, drenched in civilization, overshadowed with fear, looking back at me with some fierce and incomprehensible need, I will run.

Last summer, I went to feed the Garden Creek deer a final time. Danielle, a childhood friend, was visiting from Seattle with her four-year-old son, and neither had been within arm's length of a deer. I had not been to the Andersons' bend in the road for several years, my conscience finally winning over my love of the experience. We drove to the spot just before dusk and sat in the car waiting. No deer appeared. After about fifteen minutes, we left the car and walked around the area. In a nearby field of sagebrush, we spotted a doe and fawn feeding among a cluster of horses. We watched for a while, hoping the deer would come closer, and then we clutched our cartons of Quaker Instant Oats and climbed the barbed wire fence. After picking our way through dense brush, hands extended with imaginary offerings, we managed to come within a dozen yards of the animals before they fled into the hills.

Disheartened, we returned to the road and continued waiting. Our disappointment intensified as the deep pink alleys spreading out from the sunset changed to cobalt and then black. I tried to explain that the deer might not be gathering as often, if at all. Possibly the deer that remembered how to trust food-bearing people were so scarce that the supply of "leaders" was too depleted to keep the groups forming. Danielle packed away her video camera and we began the drive back to town.

My memories of my junior high friendship with Danielle glow with rebellion against my own loving and rule-bound family. I was enamored with her unpredictable house, its grimy counters and angry, junk-filled yard. When she moved to Seattle at the start of high school to live with her mom, I felt my one glimpse into the ragged edges of life—the moments that make breath flutter in the chest—had closed.

My most vivid adolescent memory involves Danielle and me, fourteen years old, "borrowing" her father's white Chevy truck at 2 A.M. for a joyride. We pushed the heavy truck a block from her house before starting the engine, pausing to watch a policeman drive slowly by in his shiny car. For a couple hours, we drove empty streets, pulverizing the worn gears, letting our fourteen-year-old laughter peal into the blackness. I had never felt such exhilarating, anxious freedom; I had never loved another person so fervently as I loved Danielle that night. I did not know that within a week she would come to school with a coffee-colored mark above her left eyebrow, a memento of her father's insight.

My frustration at missing the deer was greater than it should have been. My attempts to show Danielle and her son a good time had been strained, and I put a great deal of faith in the deer's ability to break the ice. For Danielle, returning to Casper was to open a condemned highway in her memory. Every familiar street and building stole another piece of her new confidence. Through all of my attempts to show them the changes in the city, Casper Mountain stretched to the south like a silent blue curse.

We are only half a mile from the intersection of Garden Creek Road and the highway when Danielle tells me to stop the car. Her voice is excited. I pull to the shoulder and Danielle rolls down her window, cooing and fumbling with her box of oats. A moment later, a small buck cautiously approaches her window. He loses all inhibition when he smells the handful of oats she is extending. Danielle holds her breath as the buck eats from her hand, video camera forgotten. From the back seat, Danielle's son reaches his fingers through the window to be snuffed. A doe materializes from behind the buck and tries to snatch a share of the food. After the buck pushes her aside, I roll down my window and coax her to my side. Every few minutes, in a fit of jealousy, the buck crosses to where the doe feeds and bumps her out of the way, taking over her position. The doe, unperturbed, walks to the opposite window and continues eating. We feed them until the oats are exhausted. Tiny fragments, blown by the deer's breath, coat the inside of the car like confetti.

Unwilling to let them go, we scrape as many oats as we can from the console and floor and parcel them out in bits. Too soon the deer grow bored and trail away toward the trees, enchantment following them from the car like vapor. Danielle overcomes her awe almost immediately and falls to giggling like a child. Her son, infected with our high spirits, bounces on the back seat and pats our shoulders with his small hands. I am staring at the city lights as we drive home, unsure how to feel.

Danielle's laughter is a warm memory in my ear, and the feel of deer lips is in my palm, but the moment is crystallizing into something that feels more like an ache than a pleasure. I know I will not be back to feed the deer. I know my youth, along with my friendship with Danielle, is transforming—in real and imagined ways—into a definite shape, one that is less painful, mutating, or brilliant than the immortal mess of childhood. I don't feel ready for this shape. If I had an opportunity to step through the looking glass and forget myself, right now I would take it—if only to let this moment continue on the other side, foot forever on the threshold, instant cereal forever stuck in my shoelaces, identity suspended while four eyes glint after me from the darkening roadside.

At the Crossroads

Gretel Schueller

SOMETHING BIG IS SNORTING and snuffing outside the tent. I jolt up from my sleeping bag and nudge my companion awake. Whatever it is, it's a heavy breather, and it's getting louder. As if to compensate, we hold our breath and sit as still as we possibly can. Eventually, the sounds taper away. I stay awake a little longer until all I can hear is the steady chirp of crickets and the occasional hoot of a great horned owl.

The next morning, I unzip the tent and immediately see the source of our nocturnal noise: a buffalo, an old solitary bull munching away on the sweet grasses of this prairie in southwestern Oklahoma. He is huge, gorgeous, and awfully near. His horns are worn at the side. He wears chaps of thick, dark fur on his front legs, and an unruly mane falls from his head over his shoulders. Where the sun hits, his chocolate coat glows reddish. I know I really shouldn't be so close. Still, I take a few cautious steps forward. Staring into his big, brown eyes, I am much more concerned with trying to imagine what he is thinking.... It's hard to believe that these stately creatures were once reduced from 60 million to a mere handful. I name him Bill.

The roads leading here to the Wichita Mountains Wildlife Refuge are lined with all things buffalo. Tourist shops peddle buffalo figures, convenience stores sell buffalo jerky, and restaurants serve buffalo burgers. It's a peculiar homage to the fact that the first attempt to save the American bison from extinction took place here. In 1907, fifteen bison took a long and bumpy train ride from New York City—where they had made their home at the New York Zoological Society—to the tiny town of Cache, Oklahoma. When the train pulled in, people from the whole countryside flocked to see the shaggy beasts.

The almost immediate success of the buffalo reintroduction prompted the creation of similar big game preserves that now make up our system of national wildlife refuges. Bill's predecessors are responsible for re-establishing buffalo populations across the country. Today the Wichita herd totals about six hundred—more than the total number of wild buffalo in the entire nation in 1900.

While driving toward the refuge from Oklahoma City, I had whizzed by cow pastures, cornfields, pecan groves, and freshly tilled fields exposing dusty, brick-red dirt. Although these open plains seem mostly empty of people and buildings, this land does not sit idle.

That's what makes this nearly 60,000-acre refuge so unusual and precious. Since its establishment in 1901, the goal has been to recreate an environment that disappeared from here long before. The slaughter was not limited to just bison. Merriam's elk, the area's original subspecies, was hunted out in 1881. The giant bronze turkey no longer gobbled along creek bottoms. The only thing still intact was the natural carpet of prairie, which escaped destruction because the rocks underfoot defeated the plow.

In 1905, President Theodore Roosevelt tagged on a few more acres to the Wichita Mountains Forest Reserve and named it the first game preserve. Restocking the land with animals that had since vanished from these parts was a vastly novel concept for the time. The bison were the first to arrive. Later, elk came in from Wyoming. Turkeys were transplanted from Missouri and Texas. Recent, and so far successful, reintroductions include black-tailed prairie dogs, river otters, and burrowing owls.

Outside the refuge, none of its valuable biological capital is visible—only a pile of pink granite rising against the flat, endless plains. The mountains seem as if they were accidentally dropped here by a giant airlift. Strictly speaking, the Wichitas would be more accurately described as "big hills," since the tallest peaks are less than 2,500 feet. But here, where these rocky shoulders, dappled in the shade of drifting clouds, loom above everything else far and wide, calling them anything but mountains could get you in trouble. The Wichitas may not win any awards for their height, but they do have the distinction of being older than both the Appalachians and the Rockies. Millions of years of weathering have rounded their once pointed peaks. Ancient faults, now eroded into a crosshatch pattern of canyons, dissect the slopes. And boulders, as big as houses, cobble the valleys.

Soon after entering, we pass a few prairie dog towns. About forty miles of paved roads cut through the refuge, allowing people convenient access to the 22,400 acres open to public use. Fortunately, for now, they are littered with only the animal variety of traffic jams. Troops of prairie dogs, perched on their hind legs, pause in the middle of the road before they continue their dash across. Herds of Texas longhorns amble in front of us. And, of course, the buffalo are pretty good at stopping traffic. Squeezing by these 1,800-pound, six-foot-tall creatures is not an option. We stop the car. I roll open my window and stretch out as far as I can, sucking in the musky scent that hangs in the air.

The buffalo lumber along, their massive heads swaying from side to side. They completely surround us and hardly seem to notice our presence. Without a pause, they continue on their way, and we watch them until their woolly bodies are just brown flecks in the distance. The buffalo roam the refuge with the confidence of ownership. This is their home again, not ours.

Our destination is Charons Gardens, a 5,000-acre section that contains the backcountry portion of the refuge. We get our permits, tank up with water, and in the throbbing heat of midday don our packs and set off, following the trails carved out by the buffalo and deer. It's only June, but already it's hot. And dry. The intermittent puffs of wind feel as if they're blowing from a hair dryer.

We enter what must be an enchanted rock garden. Orange, mint green, yellow, and white splotches of lichens are splashed across jumbled boulders—granites of creamy pinks and reds—in all shapes and sizes. The scene looks like an impressionist painting. We walk carefully, making sure not to annoy any rattlesnakes that may be hidden in the shady crevices. Occasionally, a lime-colored lizard darts across our path. A pair of speedy roadrunners, a ruby-throated hummingbird, and a shy armadillo also briefly share the trail with us.

The refuge is a true biological crossroads. Here, plants and animals of the East, West, and South merge. Woods, prairies, lakes, and desert border each other. In few other places, for example, can you see broad-winged hawks along with their western counterpart, the Swainson's. Eastern tall grasses meet and mix with western short grasses.

We step around tender pads of prickly pear cacti. Most of their crimson fruits have been nibbled away. Other cacti are also in bloom, their tissuelike flowers draping color across the dusty, muted earth. The cacti, as well as the spiky yucca plants that bristle across this landscape, are the same varieties that grow many miles further west in the deserts of Arizona and New Mexico.

And yet, as we continue on toward the timbered thickets within the canyons, it seems as if we've suddenly sped to a new spot on the planet. Here, sugar maples from the deciduous forests of the East neighbor with pecan, walnut, and sycamore trees typical of southern bottomlands. At least fourteen species of oak grow in these lowlands, including post oak, blackjack oak, and the northern extent of live oak. This forest is typical of the "Cross Timbers" that once covered central Oklahoma and marked the boundary between eastern woodlands and western plains. Washington Irving likened travel through these woods to "struggling through forests of cast iron." Indeed, they offer the last leafy refuge for eastern birds before the grasslands begin.

After three hours of hiking, we reach a plateau where the wind presses gently through the grasses, blowing green-gray into silver, and colorful speckles of wildflowers sway lazily. Some of the last untilled native prairie in the country grows here. With each step, we set off a slew of insects that magically pop out of the grass and catapult themselves to a new spot. Sweaty and exhausted, we pitch our tent under the shade of a Pinchot juniper tree.

As the sun sets, we get a bit of a reprieve from the pounding heat. The air continues to cool, and the cicadas commence their chorus. It comes in waves, undulating from a buzz of white noise to a deafening whir. Soon the bats begin their nightly exodus. Perfect bedtime music.

After meeting our new friend Bill the next morning, we are reluctant to leave camp. We keep close, watching him watching us. But we realize that we are intruders; so we try—not too successfully—

to make our presence less obvious. Nestled in the sedges and grasses near a small pond, we spy: Bill wades in the murky waters, sharing his spot with a blue heron who stops for a quick forage. I wonder if we seem as harmless as the heron to Bill.

Once the force of the noonday sun fades, we climb to one of the refuge's tallest summits, Mount Scott. Circling above us, turkey vultures playfully glide along the wind currents. From here, we can see almost all the refuge. In many ways, I suppose, this spot looks a lot like it once did. But some representatives are still missing, like black bears, gray wolves, and black-footed ferrets.

And about a million more buffalo. The Kiowa Indians tell a story about the buffalo that originally roamed here: By the 1870s, knowing they were doomed to extinction, all the buffalo remaining in the region walked single file into the depths of Mount Scott, where they remain to this day, waiting for a signal to emerge. Perhaps they'll be ready to join Bill and his herd soon.

Autumn 2001

Kimberley A. Jurney

A SINGLE LIGHT BURNS in the downstairs window at Karl Kuerner's house. It is evening, and Karl lays still in his bed, gravely ill, awaiting death. Alone on a hillside, illuminated by the harvest moon, a man sits, painting the stark image. Capturing an image. Capturing a feeling. Capturing a dark, intense world that is full of pain and tragedy.

Perhaps that sense of tragedy is why I am drawn to the famous image of a lonely house. It is a house that has experienced grief, suffering, and loss—emotions the entire country endured on September 11, 2001, when all of our lives were changed forever. It is a house that Andrew Wyeth painted, and entitled Evening at Kuerners. It is a house we all know, for many of us have left a light burning for those who have not returned.

For five years I have gazed at the painting of Kuerner's farm. It hangs above the fireplace in my home in Bucks County, Pennsylvania. Bucks County is land that is rich in history and wealth. Along the banks of the Delaware River, Indian tribes, such as the Lenni Lenape, made these woodland forests their home around 1000 B.C. and cultivated the rich farmland for hundreds of years. During the late seventeenth century, it was the Lenape who first showed William Penn and his Quaker followers the old Indian trails and paths, roads that I travel today. Neighboring towns and villages, such as Holicong and Perkasie, derive their names from the Lenape language. Likewise, the Neshaminy Creek, just a few hundred yards from my home, reflects the ancient presence of the Indians.

It was from the icy shores of Bucks County, on a snowy Christmas night in 1776, that George Washington and his Revolutionary War army crossed the Delaware River on their way to defeat the Hessians in the Battle of Trenton. It seems fitting, then, that a land so rich in history should be so affected by the events of September 11.

Situated in the southeasternmost corner of Pennsylvania, Bucks County is a blend of woodlands, lakes, mountains, farms, and historic sites. It is only sixty miles from New York City and three hours from Washington, D.C. Many Bucks County residents commute to New York, and scores of them lost their lives that fateful fall day. My husband, who spent time at the World Trade Center, lost several of his coworkers. Some of the students I teach continue to anguish over the fate of their loved ones.

How could such a tragic event have happened on such a crisp, blue, beautiful autumn morning? Like every American, I find myself having difficulty understanding the terrible events. I find myself living in fear—Will it happen again? What will happen next? What will happen to my family? What will happen to me? Why?

It is because of these unanswered questions and fear that I find myself searching for peace. Searching for a way to escape the endless barrage of images and sounds related to that September day. It is why I travel to Kuerner's farm, in Chadds Ford, Pennsylvania, today.

Fall is golden in Bucks County. The sun, no longer prominent in the Northern Hemisphere, has a way of casting shadows that only heightens the bountiful array of colors shining in the light. As I make my way to Kuerner's farm, I travel winding, tree-lined country roads—roads that were meant for horses and a simpler time. Old stone farmhouses, with root cellars and iron pumps, stand as three-hundred-year-old sentinels to the past. Some, legend has it, even contain stone-arched tunnels that connect to cellars, and were used as stops on the Underground Railroad. Golden oak trees shimmer; red maple trees are vibrant with a fire of fall color. For the moment, I lose myself and escape the pressures and fears that have been burning in my mind since that day.

It is Indian summer. The hazy, hot, and humid weather that hangs over the Delaware Valley has disappeared, and in its place this glorious season has arrived. Crisp. Clear. Clean. Overhead, trumpeting their arrival, hundreds of geese are flying. Against an azure sky, they follow age-old migratory paths that bring them to grassy green fields and blue lakes. Their silver bodies glisten in the bright sunlight. Suddenly, their call is interrupted by the supersonic sound of A-10 Thunderbolt jets screaming across the sky. They jar me from my trance and back to reality.

Willow Grove Naval Air Base is just minutes away, and since September 11 the air traffic has increased considerably. Twenty-four hours a day, Seasprite helicopters, C-130 Hercules, and other fighter jets travel over the countryside. Waking us from our sleep, shaking our home, they fly so low we can read their insignias. They are preparing for war—several local units have already been sent to Afghanistan. It is not lost to me that the geese, who are preparing for the upcoming winter, are sharing the sky with planes that are preparing for a journey of their own. A journey they also hope to end before the approaching winter.

I am approaching Kuerner's farm. Across the street is the Brandywine Battlefield. The sun blazes over the rolling green hills and beautiful countryside. A giant buttonwood tree, its white and gray marbled bark peeling like paper, casts shadows over the rises. Black gum trees, whose wood was once used during colonial times as water pipes, are elegant in their stature. Their branches twist and turn into great horizontal arms which delicately dip as if to kiss the ground. Perched among the branches, countless birds relish sour fruit. Bright scarlet leaves shine bright against brown, deeply checkered bark. Steel-gray cannons, from another war, line the bluffs— weapons from another era. September 11, 1777. The day of the Brandywine Battle. The day Washington and his army were defeated by General Howe and his British troops. The day the Brandywine River ran red with blood. The date that I am trying to forget.

Despite the hot sun and warm breeze, a chill has come over me as I contemplate the significance of the dates. September 11, 1777. September 11, 2001. I find it remarkable that I have been drawn to a place where another bloody battle was fought exactly two hundred twenty-four years earlier. Could Washington and his men have ever, in their wildest imagination, envisioned planes? Could they have pictured these planes being used as weapons of mass destruction? Could they have conceived of twin steel towers, one hundred ten stories tall, exploding and crashing to the ground? Would they have believed?

I leave the battlefield and cross the street, less than half a mile from Kuerner's farm. My anticipation grows. I walk alongside a golden cornfield with stalks towering over me. Papery to the touch, the husks crinkle and whisper with the wind. In front of me, at the edge of a grassy field, I spot a herd of white-tailed deer. Their thick coats are a winter shade of dark gray and brown; they have already molted and lost their thinner reddish brown summer pelts. Several of the deer are grazing, while others are feeding from a mass of tangled vines. The bittersweet berries are a brilliant orange color. Slowly, I approach, fearful of disturbing the deer. I crouch down at the edge of the cornfield and watch. The deer sense my presence, and most leap away, their pure white tails erect. A doe and three fawns stay behind, content to continue their feast.

Before long though, the doe becomes intolerant of my presence. She begins to march toward me. Head held high, she lifts her right front leg, pauses, and then slams it to the ground with a thud. She huffs. Her left leg lifts, pauses, and then slams to the ground. She huffs. Closing the distance between us, she continues this pattern. My heart races. Her three fawns watch—ears alert, tails at attention. The doe comes within twenty yards of me—will she charge? Surprisingly, I find myself becoming nervous.

Slowly, I begin to stand. She stops. I jingle the keys in my pocket in an effort to distract her. She comes closer. The adrenaline is racing throughout my body. We stare at each other. I lower my eyes in a submissive gesture, but to no avail. She is threatened by me. She continues to march. With no choice left, I stand—fully aware that she could leap toward me and kick me with little effort. She woofs; a loud stream of air blows from her flared nostrils as she suddenly bounds away in fear. I am relieved.

The significance of the primitive encounter hangs in the autumn air. We are alike—the doe and I—both feeling threatened in a frightening and changing world. The instinct to protect those we love is a bond we share. The doe is willing to confront me. Loved ones are fighting a war for freedom. It is what connects humans with nature.

Through the trees I can begin to see Kuerner's farm. The quiet and austere landscape Wyeth painted of his dear friend's house looks much the same. The pines Karl brought over from the Black Forest, barely seen in Wyeth's painting, now loom over the farmhouse with an additional thirty years of growth. Lush, dark pine boughs sag, as though heavy with a burden. On the ground below, a bed of russet-colored pine needles looks soft and inviting.

Walking through the trees, I am invited to look above me. Black ravens are cawing as they fly through a menagerie of gold, orange, crimson, scarlet, and purple. As the gentle southern wind blows, leaves quietly float to the forest's floor. Alongside me, leaves rustle as squirrels and chipmunks gather acorns and other nuts for their winter cache. I find a place to sit.

The house, white and peeling, has not changed. Its saltbox architecture is simple, yet pleasing. The root cellar rises forth from the ground. A small creek, descending from a waterfall, flows in front of me, its subtle sound a serenade to my weary soul. Autumn leaves drift along the current like the passing season.

I have found peace.

Autumn. A tragic season. A season of change. A season of death. A season that impacts the landscape with a powerful force. Leaves change color and then, along with annuals, die. Birds migrate in their haste to leave before winter's cold arrival. Animals scurry to stash food before it becomes scarce. Who knew that this season, the autumn of 2001, we, as well as nature, would experience such a drastic change? Who knew that our lives would experience such tragedy? Who knew thousands would die? Who knew autumn would have such a profound impact upon our lives and souls?

Yet, despite these harsh realities, there is a comfort in knowing that nature's cycle will continue. We may not know the outcome of the war on terrorism. We do not know if or when the next terrorist attack will come. We cannot know who will be the next victims of this war.

But, one thing I do know is that despite the fear and doubt I am experiencing, life will go on. Oblivious to human suffering and turmoil, the animals and birds before me will continue to prepare for winter. The leaves on the trees will fall to the ground. Trees will brave the winter with nothing but bark for protection. Karl Kuerner's house will remain. A new season will begin.

This evening as I gaze upon the painting that hangs above my fireplace, I feel warmth. The light glowing in Karl Kuerner's bedroom shines for me—it shines for all of us who have found our way home amid the pain we have experienced during this season of death. There is an intimacy in the Pennsylvania landscape to which I now belong. I look forward to the impending winter and the quilt of snow that will blanket Bucks County—for when it is removed, the seeds that have fallen this autumn will burst forth from this beautiful land and color the fields again. Nature's life cycle will continue, a promise that spring will come, and with it, a hope for peace. As always, nature and time have a way of healing wounds, and with time, both the earth and my soul will have recovered from this harsh autumn season.

The Heron's Passport

Dale Herring

THE MORNING WAS BRISK, cold enough for the metal handlebars on the bike to feel like ice. As I pedaled along the C&O Canal Trail just fourteen miles northwest of Washington, D.C., I finally saw fall. It is a season of mimicry—cracked mudflats mimicked clear, glassy water shattered by the lines of fallen maple leaves floating on the surface. Driftwood appeared as birds, and birds took on the colors of barren branches and winter scrub. I was not sure who was reflecting whose blue—the sky, or the Potomac River. The trail, built as a trade route in the eighteenth century, parallels a canal on one side and the Potomac on the other. I go this way each day on my way to work, immersed in nature less than an hour before being immersed in traffic.

As my knobby tires dug quietly into the soft earth of the trail, I smelled the musk of damp, East Coast wooded banks. Leaves from beech, birch, and box elder looked like multicolored confetti suspended in air. Fog hovered as snaking tendrils just above the water in the canal. It looked as if I had ridden my bike to Avalon, the shrouded, mystical world of pagan traditions, mythical beasts, and spirits of the forest. But no, the swirling wisps of fog appeared more as genies. They seemed to be spinning frightful tales of wishes granted after a human freed them from a bottle. Sun-drenched droplets sparkled and their very essence seemed to have a glimmering sheen. Otherworldly.

A bicycle bell rang; someone wanted to pass me on the trail. She gave no indication of seeing what I did, so I thought some more. Once I had tried to save a heron on this river—not far from here. It was then, I think, that I was given a passport to heron worlds.

I found an injured great blue heron on the river just upstream from here two months ago while I was kayaking in Great Falls National Park. The bird's long, gangly neck was the only thing above water. A ranger told me that sometimes the birds lose their footing above Great Falls while they are fishing and that they get hurt as they wash down the twenty-foot drops. I scooped the bird's body with its mangled legs onto the front deck of my kayak. It broke my heart seeing the magnificent creature so broken. I had admired great blues all my life for their incredible composure and for that mesmerizing stare that burns with a wildness born of things I've never seen, as if touched with knowledge of something so large it makes for madness. Perhaps it has visited these foreign worlds behind the shrouds of mist on the canal or past a waterfall's veil. Maybe it goes elsewhere when it nests out of site in the highest trees, or when the dark river swallows its form as it dives for food.

All I know for sure is that blue herons are most active at dawn or dusk, when one world dissolves into another. When hunting, they stand forever motionless and alone, head wound like a jack-in-the-box close to its chest, ready to spear fish. I marvel that they can understand the nature of water so well that even when they lift their tall legs out of the river, there is no ripple.

Now, I wanted badly for the bird to save its strength and heal itself. Yet, it was scared and fought me—enormous wings spreading in fits and starts, beak opening menacingly—but legs tragically thin and immobile.

When I let the heron slide off the front of my kayak near shore, it bobbed in the shallow water, getting tossed about by the wake. In a ridiculous effort, I put chunks of albacore tuna that I had brought for lunch on my paddle blade. As the heron tried to fight the paddle off, I dropped the food down its open beak. Force-feeding a heron, though, doesn't do anything except make the creature more frightened. I felt absurd and bereft. I was foreign; I didn't belong in the bird's world no matter what my intentions were.

After looking into its eyes—yellow, timeless, magnificent—I paddled away, giving the dying animal some peace. When I moved into the current, I was aware that the same moving force that gave the heron its life also caused its fall. I sunk the ends of my kayak down, rolled around, and spiraled vertically in the low-volume boat trying to understand by immersion a force that could feel no remorse, but was still innocent.

I passed a fish ladder coming in on the left. I knew that hitting the new current just right would allow my boat to slip into a watery seam, like the wing of a plane, and fly down toward the bottom of the river. Kayakers call it a mystery move, and I sent the boat, angled just so, into the whirlpool like the currents that sucked my boat down. The effect was so dramatic that it silenced thought, giving the floor to sensation. Cold pressure pushed in as I dropped three, then five and seven feet deep. I was awed by the hand of nature that was so enormous it could just flick me in my kayak toward the dark river bottom. Madness. The deeper I went, the more silent it grew, and as I looked up toward the light at the surface, the great blue heron, limp—dead—washed just two feet below the waterline, downstream. It swayed and contorted like common debris—a soggy plant or a cast-off sari from a bathing girl. I pointed the nose of my boat, still under water, up to the air and let the buoyancy send me flying to the surface. A shiver racked me.

Now, as I biked along, I couldn't shake the chill of that long-ago shiver. I have often thought that something passed between that heron and me when the wild creature died. It was like this life force that took the shape of a great blue heron became mine as it dissipated in the water. Just as I thought this, I saw a bird perched amid a dredging site on the canal. Rubber tubing, a tractor, and an empty soda can didn't detract from the strength of its presence.

It was a great blue heron, prehistoric looking, outside of time, standing like a gatekeeper in the dawn. As I passed it, I dwelled for a moment longer in the world of genies, Avalon, one of the secret places herons know. I wonder where else they go. Perhaps one day I'll be able to paddle along the Potomac, slipping in and out of heron worlds, without even causing a ripple.

Poems
(from *Buried in the Sky*)
Penny Harter

The Gravity of the Sacred

Visible and invisible,
it tethers us, wraps our limbs
in radiant linen.

It beats in our chests,
flares out to bless whatever
gets in its way.

I have seen it leap across a field
riding the wind from blade to blade
until the grass grows dim again
and lost.

Feel it knocking at your throat,
wanting to speak in tongues
about the light that even now
is flaming in your flesh
for a little while.

Snow and Ash

Of the same family,
faintly white, scattered
by the wind.

Snow repeats itself,
every flake both elder
and newborn.

Ash returns to earth—
dust to dust, translated
by the flame.

Snow will freeze,
and ash smother
on their way home.

If the dead have toys
let them have these,
ephemeral as flesh.

Let them open their arms
in that field where all things
gather for the counting
and dissolve.

It Is Hard

It is hard to sleep when the wind
keeps battering the blinds,
reminding me of other winds;

of that young child her father
pushes on a wooden swing
hung from a long dead tree,

the wind of her passage
barely rustling the smile
on his upturned face;

of driven snow and the smell
of a black dog's frozen fur,
his warm breath in the kitchen,
and the thaw.

It is hard to sleep when the wind
keeps battering our dreams
reminding us of other winds

that have done with us
what they will,
and moved on.

Cartography

I.

I thought I needed a map to the past,
one that traced on creamy parchment
the way back, the route through mist
and mountain passes that would open
into a day from childhood, relatives
crowding around a picnic table,
the sky clear blue with white clouds
suspended in place.

And then an overlay, filmy
as tissue paper or ghosts,
would show the ancestors smiling benignly,
hovering above us like guardian angels,
pleased that the potato salad was fresh,
and the chicken turning nicely on the spit.

But there is no going back, no map
to lead us through the brambles
of years, pushing them aside
so we may skip along the path
into a clearing we recognize.

II.

I get out my colored pencils,
face the empty page,
and begin a map to the future.

At first, it is black on white,
lines crossing one another haphazardly,
topography uncertain.

Slowly, I begin to color
rivers, trees, hills, and the coast
of some new continent I cannot name.
Flowers embroider the four corners,
ornate, many petalled, their leaves
rising toward the heaven of my hand.

III.

Now I draw myself, stick figure
entering an old growth forest
I have given to the mountainside.
The path dissolves into a play
of light and dark.

And the others, just arriving
here and there across the landscape,
crayons in their hands,
may become you.

Flies on the Corn
(from a story overheard at a senior center)

I.

There were flies on the corn,
black bodies, twitching legs
on the glistening gold,

and flies on the greasy coat
the fried chicken wore—
breasts, legs, thighs—

and the boy's own legs too short
to touch the floor, swinging
back and forth under the table

in the farmhouse kitchen
of the Georgia home place
as his father called it,

where the screen door
slammed and didn't shut right,
and the flies...

and somewhere down the table
his red-faced grandpa sat,
belly bulging in blue overalls,

while his two young cousins,
boys brain-damaged at birth,
played in the dirt outside the door
making bird-like noises.

II.

Years later, the boy's father,
hunched over supper, muttering
"betrayal" into his stew,
reliving his brutal boyhood
as he looked back from eighty years,

told how the boy's grandpa
invited a black family to supper,
and how for dessert, the others
came by to join his grandpa

in dragging the man upstairs
into the attic to hang him
from a beam right above
the kitchen table,
            the family table,
where the flies keep coming,
and the flypaper on the ceiling
grows dark.

Poems
(from *Cascadilla Creek*)
Zorika Petic

Horses in a Summer Pasture

They stand dozing under
an ancient oak. It is hot noon,
and they are lined up head to tail
for swishing the flies away.
A mantra of birds and clouds
circles them, and they feel it.
They leave sleep to lick
a salt block and drink from a stream.
Their coats, in late summer,
are flashes of chestnuts, blonds,
and onyx under the dappled
blowing of leaf shadows.
The flies drone around the horses,
bees drone around the goldenrods
and asters. Everything has been
said and understood in the pasture,
the way, without words,
you can hear the hidden source.

Child Half-Asleep on a Farmhouse Breeze

I remember
sumacs
next to my window,
their antlers of
velvet and lace;

seeds rustling on
the grassy sea;
snores ebbing
and flowing
along the shore

of dreams;
the pulse of wind
hypnotic before
the coming storm;
and a coolness,

a hint,
that the kingdom
would leave,
taking its self in me
as it went.

Summer Morning
Three of us chase an amber
day into the valley,
to the basswood groves.

Wind and trees make
brook notes, clean
as the brooks inside leaves.

The husk of school is far away.
At the house with a vineyard,
the man and woman louden

their unhappiness;
Guernseys in a nearby pasture
gather light from the grass.

Down the road, we pass a turtle
carting its roof of stars. We pledge
allegiance, forever and ever.

Skinny Dipping

Long ago
a friend and I skinny
dipped in a creek, because
the creek asked us to.
By a deserted railroad track.
The rumble grew closer,
and before we could modernize,
a freight train passed
within judgment.
The shame over nothing
had arrived;
we knew it and could laugh.
Louise is gone.
I can still turn to the scene
and draw from it
two young girls
in young water splashed
under a clean sky.

Tree Frog

Too many worries,
too much to do,

too few years left
to do or be.

And then a frog,
delighting in

the pond on our
swaybacked roof,

begins the
song about hours

that are leaves
leaves that are shade

shade that is water
water that is breeze

breeze water shade
hours leaves

that return
to the sky

none of it to end
but fall again.

Spring Marsh

Stars and a few raindrops
swim on the marsh.
Peeper bells ride the breeze
to someone's sickbed, filling the
room with blossom air.

From groves at the marsh edge,
spirit-towers rustle; they reach
toward the farther want
and mine. Wherever I go I'm here.

Currents

A chickadee bounces
from pine to pine as I

idle my way toward
the mailbox. On this plush
April day, we've both

taken a break from work.
The thrumming of the wind

and creek, a pulse, beats
through ours. Once,
I held a dying chickadee

and felt the electricity
slowly wane. Her feet

didn't loosen from my finger
until her breath was gone.
The wild speech exited

by the route it came,
and continued as before.

Wild Hickory

Squirrels
break
the nuts

eat what
they can

reasonably

bury
the rest

instructions
for the soil

the art
will not be
lost

how
to inherit
a forest.

Poems

Adele Ne Jame

On Forgetfulness, Late Afternoon, Kahuku Point, O`ahu
after E. M. Cioran

White flocks of the Red Footed Boobie fly low
skimming the shallows of the reef for fish.
Or they glitter silver depending
on their slant in the sun. As they turn, I see
their wings edged with black, long blades twirling,
cutting, gliding. Before each wave
collapses they burst up, timing flawless,
and scatter into the sea air. Over and over,
with arresting precision. Such hunger and beauty.
The heat of their hearts, blood pounding wildly.
It takes my breath away. Rushing
past the salt burned ironwoods,
dark skeletons, beaten down by wind,
over the broken coral that piles up here
at the point and finally bleaches clean. Stricken
with too much plentitude, the harmony of

their work and pleasure, I am caught by
the tenderness of their need,
their desperate circling for food,
and how this all wipes the mind clean—
the way secret touching in the night does,
your lover's body, the heat washing grief away
briefly. The wind picks up.
The bounty of the strong world—
a fisherman heads home
carrying his full bucket of small fish.
                          And the seabirds swoop low again,
hundreds of them! They are everywhere
and then so suddenly gone from me.

—Thanksgiving Day, 2001

Jumeirah, Midsummer

In the blazing desert sunlight, your dark body,
what this gleaming light makes perfect.
I take off my clothes too, drop them in the sand,
and follow you into the shock of the hot Arabian sea,

past the shore break—we swim into the green
swells that rise powerfully and fall.
It's all hypnotic, the moving
ocean, the hot wind whistling through
the wind towers where people are praying.

The water like your body is persuasion. And in this excess
of desert light everything I see blurs.

Only pleasure. Only breathing. And heat.
Your arms tighten around me under water,
and you are delirious with freedom
as if every terrible failure had been pulled
from your heart. You hold me, pulling me back

from my dreaming with the water, the desert
light, salt burning my eyes. But the sun-blurred
edges of the village along the Jumeirah coast gleam,
the mosque, as if lit to sunfire by angles. Floating, still

suspended together, I see your eyes
greener than the clear water flooding
around us, and sad. You know I am leaving
soon. And you are so in love with endings,
the starting up and letting go. You've arranged them

for years and your love is made more perfect
each time by the loss. There is no accomplishment,
even in the face of this beauty: the flowering
desert, the impossible light;
the empty palace far off the camel's road
lit up at dusk as if it were paradise
in the middle of nothing. The marrying in the heart
of pure contradictions, the giving in.
And always the wild figs you cup in your hands
and offer me before bed, the desert heat unrelenting.

Hiking the Native Forest
with My Grown Daughter

Suddenly the dark overgrowth opens
to a garden of tall hala—untended except by wind
and harsh rain. Here at the back of the valley
near the wildest vines, the iridescent damselfly
is doing her work, mating heartshaped
with another mid-flight. Melissa says
they're endangered, nearly gone,
so delicate in what they need
to keep going. For years not so far from here,
we lived for the summer squalls that swept in
off the bay, dumping lush rain in
thrilling slanting sheets. Perfect
young family. Our nonchalant lives. Not knowing
on either side of beauty a darkness follows. And for years
after that a woman wept, walking the rocky coast
under the dying keawe trees, the moon falling
into the sea. But this high up in late afternoon weather,
we have found the beauty of the hala groves,
hundreds of trees everywhere we turn.
Their sturdy prop roots fork into the ground as if
they could stand sacred forever. A fierce endurance
we are grateful for. Even for the rotting lau hala
that sends its rich fragrance up from the warm
damp earth. The bounty of embryonic leaf to tree.
Jeweled rain and sunlight filter down through the canopy
of our silence as we linger awhile. The air only mildly
bittersweet as I watch my young daughter
at the beginning of it all, how she carries

her new love, his tenderness like confidence
in the square of her shoulders, is light with it,
joyful as the infructescence of the schefflera
we are amazed to see everywhere
on our way down. Their arching swords of blood
berries flare like love from the treetops along the ridge.
And the wind cools our faces as we stop
dumping our packs on ground to rest before
going on to wherever else we are going.

`Opihi Picking on the Puna Coast

Two dark men ease themselves over
the high ledge, work their way down
a hundred feet to the volcanic boulders submerged
by the rising sea. As one wide wave moves,
as if in slow motion, to meet this high wall,
it falls in on itself throwing a punishing
break of white water over the man
who works the black slippery boulder to the left.
He might so easily be crushed against the lava,
the air suddenly forced from his heavy lungs.
But flat on his belly, he clings to the rock
spread eagle in the sun, white foam spilling over him.
As if born to this punishment, he holds on
working fast between waves, slicing `opihi
off the rock with hard jabs of his metal blade,
fills the mesh bag tied to his waist,
then effortlessly rises and dives, falling
for long minutes below the shining water
surfacing far away to climb the next boulder

and after that, the next with such grace
and pleasure, as if no real harm
could come of this, so that the woman
watching from the ledge begins to see it
as a kind of dance, requiring careless perfection.
So clearly here the feral heart
and air to breath or nothing at all.
The flesh straining, bruised and still wanting more.

(Note: `Opihi is a crustacean, a delicacy eaten by locals and others.)

Driving Out Our Dead

When the sun slants just so on the small palms,
on the stalky spathiphyllum and their white
blooms, like palms that are reaching up for
the morning heat, you remember then—
his body like that. A field worker,
strong, dirty from labor coming to you,
reaching over and through you,
in the damp heat and silence
of the morning wind. This is the violence
you long for, though you say nothing,
the violence that opens, at last,
the lock of yourself. So that you are wholly altered
in a way he cannot know. Every curve
of his body, every hard movement, every nuanced
movement alters you wholly. His dance,
his beating heart. The smell of mock orange,
heavy. Like his arms holding your arms
and pressing your shoulders a long time.

And later, through the curtained expanse
of his breath, you realize he is hushing
you to sleep, as though you were a child
whose name might be Katherine. Something perfect
like that. Whose father did not fly off too soon
to some war, who did not come back
mangled in spirit or give his heart
to the wrong woman. He who
did not, in return, die too young. All that,
all this. Undone, or nearly.
We are driving out our dead
the Papuans say, and who better in this fight
of love than the good man, "ya wundi,"
they say, the one who dances strongly,
whose plumes wave bravely,
whose adornment is rich around his arms,
rich around his waist and around his groin.

Four Essays

Jill Robin Sisson

This Game

I LEARNED TO SLICE FROM A LOVER. He said, as I struggled with a mushroom, move the vegetable, not the knife, or you'll cut your thumb. He showed me how to keep the pointed end down against the cutting board, and slide the cap under. Neat slices fell to the right. I felt like a clock ticking off seconds: clean, efficient. I watched the knife pivot. Things moved more quickly. Then he left me for another.

Many things have left me—some not for another, but with another: another idea, another perspective. For instance, I have learned to see the forest which surrounds my childhood home as a fragment—not a figment; it is there still—but as a fragment, a narrow crescent between our lawn and the cornfields to the north and northeast, whereas once it was huge and held us, held us all, endlessly.

I have learned to see it as a slice left from what our forefathers found when they arrived. I have learned, thanks to a course in conservation biology, that leaving this slice most certainly increased the amount of edge (perimeter) of what was once unbroken interior: trees and trees and trees for miles and miles. Do the math. Draw a square that is 6" by 6" and calculate the perimeter. Calculate the area. Now divide your square into three long rectangles, each 2" by 6". Pretend what's in between are fields, or roads, or housing developments, whatever you want. Now calculate the perimeter and area of each new rectangle. By how much has the ratio increased? This is why we no longer see an interior creature such as the wolf in Westminster, Maryland.

But we do have rabbits, squirrels, fox, deer—all edge-loving animals—all the game animals of our grandfathers. So what if we sacrifice a wolf for a couple of deer? Has it hurt anything other than the rosebush in your front lawn, browsed budless by the innocent whitetail before it can bloom? Once my lover told me he liked the edges of things, as he traced the seam of my sleeve. And it is precisely at this time, when one falls in love, where before one has simply grown up in it, that edges begin.

I should have learned to slice from my mother, long before I was making pizzas with a man twice my age. For it was she who taught me first about wholes, and pieces. My youth is marked by the things she cut: grapes, celery, bangs.

Recently I was making a recipe for chicken salad that included split grapes. I reached for one of the grapes as I cut them. The flat side against my mouth brought me back to the time when my mother knew the way I laughed and ran as I ate, the shape of my esophagus, my impatience. She sliced the grapes for my sisters and I without complaint. She also gave us celery sliced carefully into half centimeters, lightly salted, because, she says, she needed to get fiber in us. They looked like short, fat inchworms. She called them "cuttin' worms" and we believed her.

When my sister got braces, she couldn't eat our summer staple. I watched for weeks this duet at the dinner table: my sister would butter and salt her corn on the cob as my mom stood next to her, grim, waiting. Then mother slid the knife down the cob in great premeditated strokes; the corn came off in great rows. I bore the whole presentation in agony, thinking, how can it taste the same in a pile on her plate? On her spoon?

She also cut in other rooms. She cut my bangs in a half-moon. I remember the cold quarter inch of the sewing scissors on my forehead, close enough to be invisible.

But eventually we had to beg, when we were grown, when we were able to reason that an apple tasted better in eighths. This is when she began to say no...

And so did I, for to keep things pure you must eventually say no. To keep things whole you must leave them whole, digest them whole, use patience and strength, and accept a bit of bitter peel with every bite. You must not take things in doses, expect them to add up to more than they are, to cure. Think of the first time she cut for you; it was letting you go, but it made you hers.

Our forest has not become smaller. No trees have been taken in the last twenty-five years, except by gypsy moths, and these have been replaced by blackberry bushes, for a while. It's just that when we were younger, we didn't see the sizes of things. We didn't go through the forest; we went in. And if we went from one end of the forest to the other, still we were not going through; we were simply going into something larger, a place that encompassed our forest, the two cornfields behind it, the wooded corridor that separated them, and the creek in the valley beneath.

Edges make the brown-headed cowbird happy. The cowbird has evolved a unique way of ensuring that it passes on its genes. It flies around the edges of things—fields and forests—looking for the nests of smaller birds: flycatchers, finches, vireos, warblers. Then it deposits one of its own eggs in each nest it finds. This is, for the most part, unbeknownst to the host, the owner of the nest, who, when the eggs hatch, will raise the cowbird as, and often instead of, her own. The reason the cowbird doesn't pick on somebody her own size: most birds, programmed to respond to the squawking of their hungry young according to volume, feed the loudest—the baby cowbird—most and more often. Other brood parasites—the European cuckoo and the African honey guide—have evolved even more horrific ways of ensuring that they alone are raised by their foster parents. The cuckoo, just after hatching, blindly and laboriously contorts its body in a series of complex, specialized moves which result in knocking other eggs and young out of the nest. The honey guide uses its hooked bill to murder any nest mates.

Some animals have developed ways to outwit the wittiest. The yellow warbler, for example, upon finding a cowbird egg in her nest—she can recognize it—will build a new floor of twigs and gray grass and mud, covering the unwanted cowbird egg and, unfortunately, also some of her own. Warbler nests have been found with six layers of new floors, each with its own cowbird egg support.

Today, I was sitting with a two-year-old in the grass. He ordered me, "Play." I said, "What are we playing?" He said, "A game." Always needing all the facts, I asked "What game?" He replied, "This game," with more emphasis than the minister had used earlier that morning while quoting Matthew 28:6. And that is a child—the world has no beginning, no setting up; we are simply in it, playing already.

Learning to read, falling in love, these are the ways edges begin. For when you are young a story is full and never leaves— just a breath can bring it about. But a chapter already divides; it becomes tiresome, dog-eared, a stretched spine. Love can become a cliff we want to jump off of all too fast. This is how we punctuate our lives.

I am asking you to stay in it. Surround yourself with something, and not just to seek its parameters. Be a creature of the interior. Don't stretch it, but use it to its fullest extent. Don't look through it; look deeper and deeper. Continue. Make sure you are looking for more, and not for a reason.

Rules

FOR YEARS, MY MOTHER IRONED in a doorway. We tried to reduce the traffic as much as possible during these times, but it was difficult to subdue our play, and she would continually pause, look down, and warn "Watch the cord!" while we slipped through the sleeve of space from the hallway to the kitchen for a pair of scissors, or a drink, and back again.

It would have been a disaster if the iron had fallen, if the cord had tripped one of us and the hot metal hit our backs. But it never happened. It was a risky situation: one end of the board firmly anchored on the kitchen tile, the other teetering on the living room carpet, half an inch higher. But there were no disasters in my house. Or in my childhood. My mother made sure of that.

Still, there were ways we broke the order with which my mother provided us. When it would snow in the evening, my sisters and I would close the bedroom door. We would kneel on my sister's bed before an open window, fearful as the cold air poured into the room and the electric heat clicked on. In our hands we held a special, homemade kind of toy: a key tied to a long string. Taking turns, we would throw the key out the open window, careful not to let go of the string. Phht. The key would hit the snow. Thht. We would draw it back again. Over and over we tossed the key and drew it in.

We did not talk. We did not plan to play this, only caught each other and were caught until we began performing the ritual in three. In the morning, these strange tracks and their thin tails were always left unopenable, locked by late snowfall. And so we did not know the meaning of the game. At the time, its mixture of innocence and deceit seemed confusingly equal. Now the message is more clear. It was a form of travel, of meeting with a different time and place than what the order in our house contained. When the key came back it carried with it something just fallen, something that might have become old by morning. Touching it before our mother announced "School's closed!" was a sensation which we allowed ourselves, and for which we broke the rules.

We are all changelings. Or, at least, something other than what our parents suspect us to be. If not from anything else, this is from the mere fact that our expectations of our parents are incongruent with their expectations of us. We must survive; they must die. It's not that children are ungrateful; it's just that all they must do to be loved is eat, drink, grow, and later, learn. But the parent must feed, clothe, hold, and for a lifetime, worry.

It wasn't until after its extinction in 1979 that scientists realized that Britain's Large Blue Butterfly was a changeling with very specific parental needs. The pregnant female Large Blue would lay a single egg on a flower bud of wild thyme. But the flower and seeds of the wild thyme would serve as food for the hatched larva for just two or three weeks. For on the evening of its final molt, the larva would fall to the ground and wait to be discovered by a red ant, who would unwittingly provide the rest of the Large Blue caterpillar's nourishment.

As the Large Blue lay in wait beneath the wild thyme, it would produce a special secretion and exhibit behavior that would convince a passing ant that it was really an escaped ant larva. The mistaken worker ant would then carry the caterpillar into the ant nest. Here, over the span of eleven months, the caterpillar would feed on ant eggs and grubs, hibernate, resume feeding, and pupate. Then, after nearly a year in the ant nest, the Large Blue would crawl to the surface and spread its wings.

How could the ant not perceive the changeling baby, changing for all those months, and at the expense of its feigned sisters and brothers? And when do our parents perceive this of us? For from the time we are born, we are growing away from them.

I remember cutting my knee in an old barn where we were not supposed to play, and my older sister fashioning a lie for me that I carried home with pride and certainty. I remember how coming home from the creek wet eventually became our domain. It was what our mother would expect, despite the gentle threats she delivered to us as we left. And there was one sacred bet: to swing naked from a vine off a platform our father had made. For this, I received a fistful of coins—my own money, unlike the change I was given to buy specific things: a penny for the gumball machine. But I drew even from that some sort of independence; in the supermarket, I made my first swap, trading one of those pennies to a girl I did not know for a few peanuts. All of this done under cover, with a strange mixture of fear and self-righteousness, feeling I shouldn't but also I must.

Sadly, our love for our parents can never be as strong as their love for us. In the animal world, the energy parents expend on child rearing, even in something as inhuman as a fish, sometimes seems extraordinary. In South America, there are fish that actually lay their eggs out of water. Glued to leaves on low overhanging branches that the fish have jumped from the water to spawn upon, their eggs are safe from predators. But the effort does not end there; regularly, the fish splash water up at the eggs to prevent them from drying out. Sometimes the transfer of energy from parent to child is so direct, fatalities occur. During egg laying and incubation in eider ducks, females can lose up to 45 percent of their body weight. What's more, there are as many adult female deaths during the two-month breeding season as in the entire rest of the year. Fecundity and adult survival are negatively correlated in a variety of species. Female house martins who raise two consecutive broods in one summer are more likely to die the following winter than females who raise just one. In fruit flies, males and females denied mating both live longer. Although not all studies concur, the law of natural selection would predict competition within the individual between reproduction and survival, since what it selects for is fitness—which science defines as "reproductive success"—and not necessarily longevity of life.

One scientist, William Clark, believes that the phenomenon of death is itself a consequence of the evolution of sexual reproduction, without which, of course, there would be no such thing as "parents." In other words, once parents came along, so did death. By loading resources into reproductive cells, somatic cells are subject to senescence, rather than repair, and are, ultimately, sacrificed when the individual dies. Although Clark's theory is built on cells, the sacrifices parents make are often all too evident: in some species of mites, the young develop all the way to sexual maturity inside the body of the mother. Brothers and sisters mate, the males die, and then the daughters devour their mother and emerge pregnant.

Whatever the origin of death, whatever the parental expenditure, this is the bottom line: the relationship between mother and child is distinctly different than the relationship between child and mother. Mother names the child; for the child, mother has no other name.

In the 1920s, five years after it was discovered that the red ant, Myrmica sabuletti, was a host to the Large Blue, scientists made an attempt to preserve the butterfly and its host by fencing in a nature reserve. Fencing in the reserve, however, excluded grazing animals. Without grazing animals, vegetation in the reserve grew unchecked. Unbeknownst at the time to the scientists, M. sabuletti would not build nests beneath plants over five centimeters high. With their host parents absent from the reserve, the Large Blue had no one to care for its young. Although other species of worker ants were sometimes convinced by the Large Blue caterpillar's red ant larva act, these caterpillars always died or were killed when taken back to the ant nests of these false foster parents.

We are all changelings. In Grimms' fairy tale, if a changeling laughs, it will be replaced by the original infant. A mother is told to boil water in egg shells over the fire; when she does, her changeling laughs and many tiny goblins arrive. They take it away, and replace it with her original child. Is this why parents take such great pains to make their children smile?

Perhaps if we understood laughter, the Large Blue would still be fluttering over the warm, dry grasslands of Great Britain today. How could we have imagined that to confine her would save her? Instead, it belittled her, turned her polished act into a death sentence, our actions like a key thrown toward some unfamiliar door, only with no way to get it back, as if there were no strings attached.

Perhaps we should have treated the Large Blue with the same patience we give to our own children when we allow them to step over cords, ford creeks, close doors. For their ridiculous rituals and games will eventually turn to their own determined choices of lover, and vocation. We must promise to protect them, but never to enclose; we must allow things to continually open and move, or we may find them going farther from us than we ever imagined they could.

Thaw

I REMEMBER GLIMPSING the scattered, glossy pages from the bridge, the half hour I stood, knee-deep in water, reading, out of order, what men and women did. I brought the pages, singly, into focus, then thrust them, larger than life, back below the surface again. I believe a friend watched me from the bridge, too smart already to come down and read.

The water opened at the backs of my knees and closed again around the caps; when I emerged that day my legs left two holes in the creek which I would use for years, like telescopes, first, then binoculars, to look at something always too distant to understand, but gradually nearer and nearer.

In my house, you couldn't go through puberty until my mother said so. That meant waiting for her decree to do all of the things I considered steps in reaching the status of my older sisters: closing the doors of certain rooms, wearing deodorant, shaving my legs. Just about the only thing my mother couldn't command with a few words was the onset of menses. Yet there was a time when I sat with my back to the full-length mirror tacked to my bedroom door, opened my legs to a small lamp whose shade I had temporarily removed, and commanded the mass of skin that this procedure revealed, to produce.

But I can't blame my mother totally for the fact that I went through sexual maturation only with her blessing. For one reason or another, in fifth grade, I needed her to notice the two new tumors on my chest to make certain they were breasts, and so I thrust them at her while she brushed her teeth one evening and

I was leaving the bath. (This was, apparently, before the closed-door stage and, perhaps, was what justified it.) Likewise, when at the predicted age of twelve and a half I rose to find roses in my underwear, I crept not to the bathroom but to the kitchen. Once there, speechless, I thrust the rusty cotton panel, now spread like webbing between my fingers, toward my mother, who stood solidly cooking breakfast in the corner, and I waited, fixed, for her directions.

When I was a child, my family's home was full of solids. Some were obvious: bureaus, canned goods, closets packed with labeled boxes. Others were more hidden: the curious, curved metal legs and plastic wheels of the beds, on which we stubbed our toes, where we thought there was just space.

Liquids, on the other hand, were a safely guarded commodity. My family cried over spilt milk. Drinks were had only in the kitchen, Popsicles only on the porch. Even when my sisters and I were too old to share a bath, we still shared the water—the last one scrubbing in the cool, washed dirt of the second and first.

There were lapses, of course. Most of them had to do with what liquids my sisters and I could find in the forest outside our home: a tryst of trees, whose shared trunk filled after rain and stayed full for weeks. We called it witches' brew, added leaves, and stirred with a broken stick. Once, half of a gallon milk jug, half full with water, was stolen from the family dog and loaded down with cow's corn for some game. Forgotten about for a few weeks, it threw a sickening, sweet, and new but familiar smell from the back of the shed. Luckily, I removed it before being found out, and shocked, inspected the numerous primitive stems and roots on the kernels, that I, that the water, that secret ingredient, had produced.

But most of our encounters with water had to do with the stream, the same where I would later find the ripped-up girlie magazine. You see, we grew up between the east and west branches of the Patapsco River, and had only to walk a half mile north or south from our back or front door to have lunch, or an adventure, near one of them. Once, quite young, I dropped a peeled orange from the bank I picnicked upon, and watched in amazement as my sister instinctively flew downstream to retrieve it. Minutes later, I was just as instinctively biting into the fruit, heavy with creek.

Where I live today, solids are somewhat harder to come by than they were in my youth. The local children whom I teach assure me that at one time the river here did freeze all winter long and all the way across. To protect themselves from the British during the revolution, they tell me, the colonists dragged huge iron spikes out upon this river's ice. In spring, when the ice melted and the river was flowing, the spikes were still there, solidly sunk to the bottom, protecting the inhabitants of the coastal towns by threatening to pierce the hulls of any ships that dared to venture near them. And, the children relate, well versed in their local history—which also happens to make a good story—there were chains put across the river, with links three feet long and six inches thick. And then they throw out the nouns: the chains and the mountains and the spikes kept the towns safe, they say. But I walk to the river in winter today and watch it pouring through patch-ice, shattering clear, brittle surfaces just two feet from its banks.

Solids are somewhat harder to come by here. Supposedly, just as at home, there are frogs that freeze in these hills—gray tree frogs, who hibernate under a bit of soil or log or leaves. When the temperature dips too low for too long, ice forms under their skin, around their stomachs; nearly half of the water in their bodies becomes solid. I search for these little nuggets of life, safe and still, adapted to waiting, and behaving, and enduring thaws and freezes, but I can't find them.

For I must go home for solid things, imagining the somewhat familiar names of the roads that will take me there in my father's voice, to prevent myself from becoming lost: Western Run, Tufton Avenue. Then, somehow, their exits become clear, fog lines defined, intersections meet. Once home, I creep through my parents' house, secretly lifting, raising, and lowering like weights the solids that I know will be there: potatoes on a shelf in the basement, in my father's drawer two shiny pink cuff links on tiny green pillows; also, a cracked leather case containing the family's only set of nail clippers. In the hall closet, three irons. A piano and organ in the living room.

When I was a child, I could not travel far enough, could not figure out where the west branch of the Patapsco River came from or went to no matter how fast I walked before dinner. Nor could I imagine how fluid my body must have seemed to my mother and father, like a spilled drink escaping carelessly and swiftly from its container from the instant I was born; for to me it seemed straight and thin and flat, and could not change fast enough. Now, I feel like I can't stop myself from going, long for those icons of history to keep me in, those matriarchal decrees, the rules that drew clear boundaries between the forms that matter could take and the places it could be. I long for something to cradle, to hold or to hold me, a cuff link, or even heavy curtains to hang on a picture window. But mostly, I long for those two holes I put in the creek long ago not to close, but to heal, to bring into focus once and for all what the river had, and has, to show me.

Homing

WE ALL HAVE A SENSE OF HOME. For most of us, it is the place where we spent our childhood. For some of us, home grows, and can include where we met love, or learned something new. For others, home remains only the place where we, ourselves, grew.

Animals also have a sense of home. Some of them—especially birds—have quite an extraordinary one. Migration, in which birds fly between seasonal homes along the same path, can be amazing in itself; the Arctic tern travels nearly forty thousand kilometers twice a year, virtually from one pole to the other, a far greater distance than most humans will travel in their lifetimes. But a greater mystery than migration is the quality of "homing," or a bird's ability to return to its home from an unknown area over an unknown flight route.

Most people are familiar with the homing pigeon, a domestic bird used for sending and receiving messages to and from base camp in World War I. Interestingly, the rock dove, from which the homing pigeon was bred, is a nonmigratory bird with very little homing ability. But if a homing pigeon can be bred from a virtually sedentary bird, all birds must exhibit homing to some degree, and terns, gulls, cowbirds, starlings, and swallows—some of which may make their home in your backyard—can find their way back to their homes in astonishing circumstances.

In two early experiments, noddies and sooty terns were transported by steamers from the Tortuga Keys between Florida and Cuba to a variety of points never before visited by the birds along the Atlantic and Gulf coasts. A bird taken 585 miles from its nest returned in just under four days; one taken 855 miles away was back in just over six ("Homing of Birds," 1971). But more fascinating than when the birds returned is how they did it.

At first, it was commonly thought that the birds were simply retracing the exact route used to take them away, using either visual cues, or an "inner ear guided" sense of direction. To disprove this, scientists gathered a sample of starlings, chloroformed them, placed them in boxes, and rotated the boxes on phonographs during transport from their homes. When the birds were awakened and released, even after this dizzying experience, nearly 100 percent found their way back to the nest ("Homing of Birds," 1971). Another theory held that birds used a "magnet" located in their brains to follow the earth's natural magnetic fields. More ingenious scientists stepped in, releasing pigeons with strong magnets fastened beneath their wings in order to confuse them. Did they make it home? You bet, in spite of the extra weight ("Navigation of Animals," 1971).

Although, in general, they excel at it, birds are not the only animals with homing ability. Salamanders can find their way back to a favorite section of stream from up to one mile away ("Navigation of Animals," 1971). Even box turtles, normally thought of as slow and impeded travelers, have found their way back through unknown territory when released from one to two miles from their homes (Carroll, 1996). A female wolf in Montana, after being implicated to have killed a rancher's heifer, was drugged, taken 160 miles from her mate, and released, yet found her way back to her mate's territory, and the disgruntled rancher's property, in eleven days (Chadwick, 1998). In addition to the ability to find their homes against great odds, these animals must also have an uncannily strong motivation to look for them, for they persevere even when the territories they are placed in could presumably meet their basic needs.

More recently, scientists have posited that it is a combination of abilities, including magnetic sensing and navigation by the sun and stars, that allows birds to home so efficiently. How odd that the simple stars, the objects that first led men away from their homes and into new worlds, turn out to be the clue that animals all over the globe are using to return to their homes, after being displaced and misplaced by humans, not in the experimental arena, but in the economic one. Perhaps that is where humans strayed, literally: passionately overdeveloping their skills in exploration and, as a consequence, losing the knack for getting home. Like Odysseus, who sailed the sea for ten years before returning to the house where his wife and dog faithfully awaited him, we have covered the corners of the earth, discovered and uncovered all of her habitats, and now find ourselves desperately trying to recover them.

So let's begin to think of home. And let's imagine that our own sense, like the birds', is something grand that we are not fully conscious of, some science at work within us, leading us back to earth from the air and the sea. Let's believe that there is some faultless guide steering us home, and hope that if we are not there now, we soon will be.

Works Cited

Carroll, David M. 1996. *The Year of the Turtle*. New York: St. Martin's.

Chadwick, Douglas H. 1998. "Return of the Gray Wolf." *National Geographic,* May, pp. 78–79.

"The Homing of Birds." 1971. *Audubon Nature Encyclopedia*. Philadelphia: Curtis.

"Navigation of Animals." 1971. *Audubon Nature Encyclopedia*. Philadelphia: Curtis.

Hunting the Invisible

Gretchen Dawn Yost

I ONCE VOWED TO MYSELF that if I ever hit a deer, I would quit driving. The remainder of my life would be arranged to persist on foot or bicycle. I sneered at people who spoke regretfully about their damaged vehicles but failed to mention the deer, the other consequential side in a collision of lives. In my adolescence I offered long-toothed snarls to overweight men in beat-up trucks, rifles slung lazily in their rear cab windows. I bought mustard greens and organic tomatoes, ate couscous seasoned with sweet basil and chives. My groceries came from dimly lit shops with wooden counters and brown paper bags that smelled of incense. I gave little thought to the flesh and bones of wild animals. In that cast-off life of mine, God's will begged the immortality of deer.

At some point on the precipice of change, I packed my bags and loaded my three-banger Geo Metro to the hilt with thermal underwear, cross-country skis, books and journals and drove the icy, eastbound road to the mountains of Wyoming. I spent the winter snowed-in with solitude and an absence of human noise. Spring came plump and lush like a fertile moon over sagebrush plains. And gray-crowned rosy finches carried summer on their salmon-brown wings all the way to the craggy mountaintops and back down again. Before I could shake my head and blink, I felt a deep pain in my abdomen, a yearning in my bones.

With the advent of autumn, trucks came pouring out of the woods and plains, proudly displaying the body parts of elk, deer, moose, and antelope. Dizzy with sickness and hunger all at once, I became like a scavenger on wolf-kills: an elk steak here, a deer burger there, some frozen bricks of moose from the woman at the post office. At a baby shower in October, women spoke of blood up to their shoulders, of seasonings, tenderizer, and freezer wrap. They spoke of stews and chili and the long winter ahead.

In this land where they grow hay and cows and not much else, there are things that make sense to my body and others that do not. I dropped mustard greens and couscous for a knife with a sharp edge. Brown paper bags that once held my subsistence gave way to a sleek, walnut-stocked mountain rifle. I had tasted the exuberance of these wild lives, but I wanted to know their deaths, the fullness of that kind of sorrow. I wanted to roll the roundness of life and death on my tongue, and savor it.

It wasn't a morbid curiosity that I held, not even a stubborn insistence to be self-sufficient, but more of a desired completion. I wanted the direct experience without mediation. I wanted to know what I was eating and how it came to die. I wanted to interact with an animal in the most ancient, primordial way. I wanted, through the hunt, to become part of an animal and for that animal to become part of me and part of my story.

Tracking and stalking a deer I was sure I could learn, with patience. But whatever came after that was a mystery to me. The gutting and boning-out, even the shot itself, I knew nothing about. I begged some local boys to take me hunting, to show me how it's done. They grimly instructed me: "if you see something, shoot it." Another brotherhood of hunters matter-of-factly explained to me that a vegetarian wouldn't be able to handle the sight of blood. I wanted to remind them that I am a woman, that my alliance with blood is as old as the moon. I didn't ask them again.

Eventually I did find someone who would take me hunting, among other things. Our love affair began during some late summer rains when we tucked inside a 1950s camper trailer nicknamed the "Silver Bullet," keeping each other warm and smiling. It was like pulling teeth to get him to talk about almost anything, but when I asked him about hunting, words and stories flowed from his mouth like warm honey. He talked about the habits of deer and of squirrels. He told me about his first deer hunt when he was thirteen, how he had to shoot seven times, how he cried and begged the deer to die, and how he still carries seven bullets to this day. Lying next to him, I listened with my eyes wide open. I wondered what I would have thought of this man five years ago. I wondered what I would have thought of him one year ago.

We spent the winter together, telling stories, sharing food, catching up on each other's pasts.

Autumn came slowly, like a tired old man shuffling across the kitchen floor, proving to be in no hurry to turn the heat off. In the absence of stormy winds aspen leaves had plenty of time to change color, transforming the woods into a patchwork of greens, yellows, oranges, and reds. I was target practicing nearly every day, learning a new kind of meditation. I would concentrate on my breath—*breathe in, breathe out, breathe in*...squeezing the trigger on the breath out as though the bullet was an extension of my exhalation. Learning not to flinch, I focused on flowing into the shot, trying hard not to close my eyes and jerk my arms—an extraordinary task when expecting a sudden, ear-ringing crack and the butt end of a rifle to hit my shoulder like a domineering older brother. And yet, with my rifle resting on a two-legged support, I was good. I could hit my mark.

Mule deer season opened unceremoniously on a hot and sweaty September day. I was excited to hunt but Adam said we should wait, that it was too hot and the deer wouldn't be moving; the bucks wouldn't be chasing does. "They're like us," he said. "They don't get as horny when it's hot out." But the weather was not turning and excitement was getting the better of both of us. We took to hunting a small area close to home in the evenings, after work.

By the time I actually began hunting, I had created a number of handicaps and restrictions for myself. I would not shoot at any animal over two hundred yards and preferably not over one hundred. I would not attempt an offhand shot; I would only use the bipod support. And I would only make a broadside shot: that deadly spot just behind the shoulder where bullet passes through heart and lungs. I convinced myself that these restrictions were an ethical acknowledgement of my own limitations and skill. But I realize now that they also served as a convenient excuse for not killing, for not pulling the trigger.

Adam and I would walk together, coordinating our footsteps so that we created the noise of a single hunter. For many afternoons I walked behind him, paying more attention to when and on what my foot would land than I did to my surroundings.

Then, one evening shortly before dusk, Adam spotted a buck about two hundred yards away. He had not yet noticed us. We dodged from the semicover of one sagebrush to another until we were within one hundred yards. Still, the buck did not move. I crouched behind a large sagebrush on the crest of a small rise and Adam settled himself behind me, his chest to my back. Noiselessly, I extended the legs of the bipod. I positioned my body so that the flesh of my arms just above my elbows met the flesh of my inner thighs just above my knees, allowing my propped-open legs to steady my arms. Slowly, I raised the rifle to meet my shoulder, stretching my neck forward to rest my cheek on the cool, walnut stock.

He was a little buck, grazing in the shadows of a stand of yellow-leaved aspens. I put the riflescope on him; he was standing broadside but he seemed far away and I whispered so to Adam.

"No, no, he's just small," he whispered back. I thumbed the safety forward, held the crosshairs steady just behind his shoulder, my index finger cocked on the trigger. He was grazing, moving forward. I heard Adam breathing heavily behind me, his body trembling next to mine.

"He's too far away," I whispered again, still following him with my rifle.

"No, no, he's not far. You can make the shot."

I continued to keep the crosshairs on him, but relaxed my finger. I knew then that I would not kill that buck. I grasped at the first reason to put my safety back on, and when two thin aspen branches obscured his brown body ever so slightly, I told Adam that the limbs were in my way and I could not shoot. Not that day, not that deer.

Something was missing; it never felt right. He wasn't mine to take. Something never came together between that deer and me. I could not give him that sheer and divine attention from one being to another. Although I had learned infinite amounts from hunting with Adam, I knew I had to break away and go alone. The presence of another person proved to be awkward—like a third wheel or a ménage a trois. Hunting is an interaction that's really meant for just two—the focused engagement of hunter and hunted.

We awoke to thin, light snowflakes landing gently on the slanted windows of the skylight, like hundreds of ballerinas silently falling to their tiptoes. I quickly rolled out of bed, ran down the twisted loft stairs and out the front door to scan the western horizon. Clouds. White, dark gray, deep blue. The air held that distinctive, foreshadowing aroma of moisture infiltrating dry, parched soil. It would snow—or rain—most of the day. The night before, we had planned to have a workday; to cut and split a few cords of firewood, take down the gutters, put away the garden hose. Instead, we swallowed the morning leisurely, all the while keeping a watchful and nervous eye on the composition of the sky, hoping with a gut-like faith that the sun would not break through. As though our patience would reward us, Adam and I spent the early afternoon doing our chores around the cabin, so that it was only a few hours before sunset that we changed into our camouflage clothing and gathered our backpacks and rifles.

At the beginning of the hunting season, my backpack contained all the necessities of survival: knife, matches, backup lighter, firestarter, space blanket, headlamp, extra batteries, first-aid kit, rain jacket, compass, map....The camera was the first to go. It had seemed presumptuous to hunt with a camera in my possession. Then—thinking that the more hardships I had to endure, the better my hunt would be—I dropped the firestarter and space blanket, next the extra batteries and matches. And eventually, in that manner, superstition pushed necessity out of my pack.

The contents were replaced or altogether forsaken. I then carried only a card with a pressed yellow cinquefoil flower that Adam had given me, my silver Indian bracelets representing Rain and Bear that I normally wore but didn't while hunting since they reflected light, a broken necklace from the Philippines that was said to ward off evil spirits, and Pipsqueak—a little mouse made of denim and stuffed with rice that my grandmother had sewn for me when I was five—whom I had wrapped carefully in a pink bandana. Of the survival gear, I managed to retain only the compass, lighter, and knife.

Adam parked his truck in the ditch beside the Forest Service fence, and from there we walked up the sagebrush-covered slope. When we reached the first bench where sage met pine, we decided to split up. Adam would take the high route, hunting along the top of the ridge where, he hoped, the big bucks would be hanging out. And I would take the lower route, traversing fingers and gullies through a mix of sage, pine, and aspen.

It was still lightly snowing, and through the clouds the sky was a deep, warming shade of lavender. I decided to take it slowly, very slowly. The fresh moisture softened the fallen leaves enough that I could easily pad my way around the dried mule's ears plants that were still so brittle they sounded like shattering glass even when brushed with a pantleg. I turned to glance at the Gros Ventres range behind me. The Big Bellies. A mountain range pregnant with enormity and beauty. A thick strip of that lavender sky ran through their midsection like a satin cummerbund, leaving their peaks and bases white with the fresh snow.

The first two ridges and gullies I crossed were so thick with the low branches of subalpine fir that the chances of spotting a deer were minimal. Still, I walked painstakingly slow, pausing often to listen, look, and smell.

After rising out of another narrow gully, I noticed ahead of me a large, open stand of leafless aspen. I remained in the protection of the fir trees while thoroughly glassing the space in front of me. The floor of this wide, shallow valley was thickly carpeted in yellow and orange leaves, as if a giant had spilled a pocketful of gold coins all at once. And the bright, white, aspen trunks shot out of the forest floor, straight yet crooked, like lightning.

Suddenly, I heard loud, shuffling steps through the leaves to my right. I froze. Recalling what Adam's father had told me about such clamorous noises—*it's either a moose or a squirrel*—I tried listening through my feet, weighing the sound more precisely. The noise had quick, broken movements, light and sticky. Squirrel. I sighed.

It was there, underneath those fir trees, that I closed my eyes, took a deep breath, and imagined myself as a deer. A light-footed doe, maybe. I took a step when I thought she would, paused while she ate some dry grass, and nosed around a low tree limb.

She took another step, and another, to get to that other patch of grass. She grazed there for a while—I don't know how long. She lifted her head while chewing; positioning her ears to confirm that all that racket was, in fact, only a tree squirrel. Silently she moved toward the spring, stopping there only briefly before continuing on. She would pause in one place for so long, then take one step further, sometimes three, sometimes twelve.

I opened my eyes and found myself in the middle of the open stand. The snow had slowed to a sprinkle and then to cold, moist air. I was on a game trail.

I continued to move intermittently, working my way to the ridge on the other side. Looking down into a narrow willow bottom below me, I spotted a cow moose and wondered if she had a calf with her. She saw me, or at least looked my direction in that defiant way as if to say *I know what you're up to*. I moved farther up the valley, out of her way so I wouldn't be a threat.

At the top of the valley I discovered a low gap crisscrossed with deer trails and scat. I sat down until it was close enough to sunset that I thought I should hunt my way back to the truck before it became too dark. I started my way down the middle of the aspen valley. When I got closer to where I had seen the cow moose, I put some weight back into my feet, forgetting about hunting altogether and worrying more about getting stomped by a defensive mother moose. I moved down the hill at a sloppy, ungainly pace, kicking up aspen leaves as though plowing through an office littered with loosely crumpled papers.

I slowed when I approached the willows, where I had last seen her. Then I heard something. Something big shuffling through the leaves. The sound was loud, weighted, and carefree. Moose.

I scanned for the unmistakable coffee-brown body so that I could skirt around her, but saw nothing. Nothing, until I caught, in the corner of my eye, a light brown deer. He blended so well into the colors of the fallen leaves and the browning willows that my mind's eye, searching for a large, dark-bodied moose, nearly failed to see him. It had been this deer making all that clamorous noise.

I thought for sure that he saw me, or heard me, and would soon bound away, but he didn't. He wasn't far, yet in the dimming light of day I could not tell, absolutely, if he was a buck. Doe season had already passed in this area and our tags were eligible for antlered deer only. I thought I saw antlers, but raised my binoculars to be sure. Buck. Another youngster, his forked antlers displayed a third tine barely as long as my thumbnail. He was grazing intently, pawing at the aspen leaves to get to the grasses underneath. I sank almost ridiculously behind a few aspen saplings, their thin branches covering my body about as well as a string bikini.

I found myself struck dumb with disbelief that this wild, elegant creature had not yet noticed my loud, clumsy self. And yet, at the same time, I understood that he was working his way toward me, to bisect my path perpendicularly. If he continued, it would be a clean, broadside shot. I wasn't going to force anything. If he were to turn and run, or just turn and stare, that would be fine. There would be no shot. But if he were to stride, broadside, in front of me, I would shoot.

Kneeling, I extended the legs of the bipod, slowly, silently. My breathing was shaky and hesitant, as though breathing cold, winter air. I tried to steady myself while teetering on my kneecaps in a half-crouched, half-kneeling position. Anything else and I would give myself away. He was coming, too fast, I thought at first. But then, he slowed in front of me.

In those last few moments he continued his slow stride forward, uncovering grass with his hooves. I could almost feel the ripple of his shoulder blade muscles as I focused just behind them. Right then, at that instant, I squeezed the trigger.

My heart leapt into my throat.

·He sprang up and ran like hell, for fifty yards, then dropped forcefully to the ground.

I waited, my heart pounding blood loudly through my ears. I raised my binoculars, searching for movement. He was still. He lay on his side, his head propped up by antlers driven into the ground, his nose to the sky.

Only then did I remember to breathe.

I forced myself to approach him slowly, the blood in my legs pumping, throbbing, trying to race ahead of me. As I drew nearer, I was struck by the familiarity of a thing up-close. Intimate. The secrets held in an eye.

I tested him, to be sure there was no life left struggling inside of him, with my foot, then my hand. I breathed a nervous sigh of relief.

Suddenly and without thinking, I fell to my knees. Words of prayer flowed so spontaneously it's difficult to remember their combination. *Thank you for giving your life to sustain my own. May your kind always bless this earth with your beautiful presence.*

Death, it seems, has dined at the head of the table during the last year.

Recently, my grandmother died. Her plane was not hijacked. Nor did a collapsing building crush her fragile bones. A few months earlier, she had taken herself off the blood thinners that kept the rivers flowing through her veins. The downhill side came suddenly, surprising even her as her home stood witness to the last-minute dealings, the wet ink on the family genealogy chart.

She left us a legacy of artwork. Her bright, detailed paintings the underscore of her life, punctuated by her independence and perfection, the stubbornness of her strength.

She was a difficult one to lose. We shared the same birthday; the same high, wrinkled forehead; the same preference for silver and turquoise. Her loss left a stream of questions to which no one had the answers.

But emptiness quickly folds in on itself. And in the wake of my grandmother's death, I feel the enormous weight of her life resting more heavily on my shoulders. I hang her paintings, I wear her rings. I wait for someone to ask about these things, so I can tell them. So they will know.

Death is a contract with the living.

The visible, like a dance, is choreographed around the invisible. Life, around death. Grace is to acknowledge this partnership, to grab the other by the hand and waist and swing together. To ignore it is to collide, to bump and stumble and fall.

Some people say we don't need to hunt. We have grocery stores. I wonder where they think the food in those stores comes from. The freezer in the back storage room? We fail to acknowledge that death sustains us. We avoid it; we buy our meat in sterile stores, coming to us in such a way that it is indefinable what animal built those muscles in its walkabout through life. Or, like I was, we eat only the plant life, forgetting about the rabbits who fall prey to the tractor when tilling the land for soybeans, or the small squirrel lives crushed beneath the tires of a truckload of organic tomatoes. How, in such a rounded earth, do we separate life from death? Where do we draw the line?

I like to think that I do need to hunt. That my very physical existence needs a coexistence with deer—with their predators and prey, their woods and brushland, their large swaths of unfragmented, unmanipulated land.

With the death of that first deer, I became a hunter. And with those words of prayer, I made a vow. Upon my shoulders was granted the great gift of responsibility. I took on the nearly unbearable weight of protecting that which sustains me. I entered into a contract. A commitment. A marriage, with deer.

Some hunters seem to be more concerned with maintaining their right to bear arms than maintaining the habitat of the very animals they hunt. Betrayal. They are not keeping up with their end of the bargain.

In our culture, we seem to forget that the earth is round; that the universe moves in circles. Linear thinking, linear behavior, is a straight path to an end. And a path to an end is one of destruction.

We need to remember once again how to dance in circles. That a relationship of taking is also one of giving. What do we sacrifice? What do we give back?

We bump, we stumble, we fall.

The sun was sinking quickly and I didn't have a flashlight. Standing up, I brushed my hands together and ordered myself to get pragmatic. I dug my knife out of my pack. I had seen Adam gut an antelope, once. In my hunter's safety class we had watched a video of a man field-dressing an elk. I thought I knew how to do it.

Propping the buck's hind legs open, I made a short upward slice starting at his groin. With pursed-lip concentration, I continued to make a series of small, ineffective cuts.

As a child, my closest neighbor and best friend's dad was a duck hunter. We would wait for his pale yellow pickup to pull into the driveway and marvel with a degree of sadness at the colorful feathers of the ducks he had lined up evenly on newspapers. We would poke at their cold, stiff bodies, then wince, yanking our fingers back close to our hearts as though we'd been bit.

This is how it was, that first time; with every cut and tear, I pulled my fingers back and held them to my heart.

I cut nearly halfway to his rib cage when I realized that I was only cutting hide and mesentery. There was still a whole layer of abdominal muscle I needed to get through. I felt stupid, surprised by my biological ignorance. Dark was rapidly approaching. I started whimpering, blinking back tears from my eyes as I tried to focus on my pale fingers guiding the knife blade through the deer's belly.

I sliced through the thin, red muscle only a few inches before his stomach sack started pressing through the hole I had created. I cut more, careful not to puncture anything in his gut. I knew that it was in this process that meat gets spoiled and tainted. I knew I needed to get those hot guts out quickly, so the meat could cool down. As I cut the last few inches up to the point of his rib cage, his stomach, bladder, and intestines rolled over the left side of his body cavity, onto the ground. I could taste my salty tears as they flowed down my cheeks, and then down his slick, white stomach, nearly glowing in the fading light.

When I reached deep inside his body cavity to pull out the other organs—heart, liver, lung—I realized with horror that everything was still attached. It was dark inside, I felt blind. I tried to feel my way around blood and rib cage, and tender organs. I was afraid to cut at anything in the dark. I was afraid I'd puncture his guts and end up marinating the meat in acidic juices. I stopped. On my knees, head bowed, I rested my knife hopelessly on my thigh.

I began to think it was a mistake. That this deer had died for nothing. That I had ruined him, ruined his flesh because I would not be able to finish the job I had started, not in the dark. I felt irresponsible, wasteful. I should have known better than to try it alone, my first time.

I had to go back. I had to get a flashlight, or a lantern. Grabbing my backpack, I slung my rifle over my shoulder and headed downhill. Bawling, sniffling, stumbling my way back to the truck, I managed enough sense to unload the magazine of my rifle. The shells clanked noisily in the cargo pocket of my pants as I tripped on the low gnarls of sagebrush, ankles wobbling, knees shaking. This was my adrenaline, a mother's frantic worry: was this death for nothing?

Finally, as I topped out on the last crest before the hill dropped down to the truck, I heard Adam calling my name. I called back. In the darkness of the new moon, I could barely see a figure approaching me. I was bawling uncontrollably. I bowed my head and cried into his shoulder, I asked why he had not come.

"What do you mean?"

"You said you'd come if you heard a shot," I mumbled.

"You shot at something?"

I nodded into his shoulder.

"What happened," he asked carefully, "did he get away?"

"No," I sobbed, "I couldn't gut him."

Adam would spend the next hour convincing me that I hadn't ruined anything, that the meat would be fine. He had killed a deer too. We would come back, within an hour, complete with frame packs, plastic bags, lanterns, and dog. It would be a long night. Adam would help me bone-out my deer into muscle groups: a task that takes a biologist's precision and a lover's patience. We would sing songs, loudly, to ward off the invisible bears waiting to feed on our gut piles. We would not sleep that night.

As we worked well past dawn processing and packaging meat on the kitchen table, I thought of how I would look forward to winter, when I would pull a tightly wrapped white package out of the freezer labeled GY DEER LOIN 01. An odd combination of letters to symbolize such an exquisite animal, a phenomenal engagement—this ancient thing called the hunt.

I understood, with quiet gratitude, that I had taken that deer's life with all the savage force of a hungry spirit.

In this dry land of extremities, I still long for the fecundity of greens, the dim humidity of vegetables and brown paper bags impregnated with incense.

I see roadkill in a whole new light. A senseless death, the lack of involvement, of interaction, of engagement. The lack of a hunt. The year before I became a hunter, I hit a deer. In the thick lodgepole forests of our first national park, in the blue light of dawn, a fawn leaped out of the woods and into the side of my little car. I stopped and walked up to him, a pool of congealed blood lay by

201

his head. The tangle of his long legs scurried, as though trying to run away as I approached. I knelt down, stroked the side of his head, stroked gently around his eye and whispered to him, asking him to let go. His legs slowed to silence, and I witnessed the life pass through his small body.

The servitude I owe this animal who has now become woven into the very fibers of my own muscles is overwhelming.

Death is a contract with the living.

Can I demonstrate this kind of grace? The grace of deer?

What We Found

John A. Murray

I.

MANY YEARS AGO my parents lived at 2146 Eighteenth Avenue in San Francisco. The house is still there. You can see it. Like most homes in that residential area, it is what would be called a town-house elsewhere: a street-level garage over which the carpenters of a century past raised a single long floor. In back of the house there was a walled garden. Even in late December, when I would come to visit, the pale red roses would be blossoming. Everything in the garden—trellis, leaves, thorns, flowers, seashells, rocks, ferns—was perpetually wet from the fog. This was a good time in their life. During the week my father worked downtown at a job he loved, and my mother, who was an artist, painted regularly at the conservancy. The weekends were reserved for expeditions to places around San Francisco: the Marin Headlands, Point Reyes, Napa Valley.

In April of 1986 the Friends of Photography organized a one hundredth birthday celebration for Edward Weston (born March 24, 1886). At that point Weston had been dead for twenty-eight years. Like all great artists, he was, notwithstanding the minor inconvenience of cremation, still very much alive. The event, sponsored by family and followers, was held in Carmel, where Weston had spent most of his career. My parents were admirers of Edward Weston, Ansel Adams, Imogen Cunningham, and the other members of Group f.64. Naturally they had to drive down the coast to attend. The event would also afford them the chance to finally meet Charis Wilson. It was in Carmel that Weston had spent fourteen years with Charis, who was his model and wife during his most productive period. Oftentimes the two had worked together in the California desert, trying to uncover the resonances between the landscape and the human form. At times they achieved images of tremendous power and virtuosity. In her 1998 memoir, *Through Another Lens: My Years with Edward Weston,* Charis wrote that, "Edward was...a robust lover of life...a man who found the world endlessly fascinating. With his camera he pored over it, probed it, and sought to comprehend it, and to render for others its beauty, complexity, and inexhaustible mystery."

Toward the end of the first day, a few of the guests—Charis Wilson, Virginia Adams (Ansel's widow), the three Weston sons (Brett, Cole, Neal), my parents—moved from the gallery to the old wood-framed house on Wildcat Hill. This was the home in which Weston had lived with his wife and many cats. A tour of the grounds followed, and my father tells the story of the unusual darkroom in which Weston worked. At one point during the visit he asked Charis Wilson if it would be possible to see the room where Edward Weston died. Weston had suffered from Parkinson's disease during his final decade. On the last morning of his life—January 1, 1958—he had somehow raised himself up into a chair and turned the chair to face east, toward the rising sun. That is how the seventy-two-year-old artist passed away, facing the dawn. Although Weston's body had been destroyed, his spirit was still drawn to the light of the sun that had created him. After Charis led my father to the room, he asked if he could photograph the chair, which still faces east. Charis graciously gave her consent. That photograph is among his treasures.

Over the years, growing up in such a household, I often studied the daybooks of Weston and the nude figure studies that he and Charis made as they explored the sand dunes around Stovepipe Wells in Death Valley and the Oceano sand fields near San Luis Obispo. All of these were eight inch by ten inch black-and-white contact prints that Weston, always a purist, refused to enlarge or alter in any way. At such times I would find myself wondering if I could ever find someone, as Weston did, with whom to collaborate on such a project. It seemed to me the Painted Desert was better suited as a landscape than the Mojave Desert. For one thing, the slickrock provided a closer analogue to the human form. The flesh-hues of the sandstone similarly offer a useful metaphor. Color film could also be used to advantage. Most importantly, no serious work of this nature had ever been done before in that part of the Southwest. The possibilities for original work were unlimited.

II.

One spring several years ago I was out in the Red Rock Desert in an area that is now known as the Grand Staircase–Escalante Canyons National Monument. At that time it was BLM grazing land—unfenced cattle allotments, seasonal line camps, wood corrals, and empty cactus desert. I had parked my vehicle and raised my tent among the junipers near a place called Twenty-Five Mile Wash. From there I was well situated to explore a vast country that extended from Davis Gulch on the south to the Kaiparowits

Plateau to the west. Every day was different. Some days I hiked from dawn to dusk, exploring the beautiful canyons. Other days I remained in camp, watching the clouds, napping, cleaning my cameras, and writing. I was happy to be far from civilization and its discontents, and I felt fortunate when I recalled other times in my life when I hadn't enjoyed such freedom. I was alone and happy and I would sit there and think that no one, at least no adult, had the right to be that content. In retrospect, I see now that it was also a healing time—not long before I had stood in a hospital room and watched as the doctors had tried in vain to save my mother's life.

Every three or four days I would drive the thirty miles back to Escalante—sun-darkened, smelling of sage, a bit of the deer in my eyes—to buy fresh provisions at the grocery store on Main Street. While in town I would call my nine-year-old son in Atlanta and my father in Denver. Whenever I am away on a trip my father picks my mail up at the post office, and then opens and reads the letters to me over the phone. One night he read a letter from a woman in Albuquerque who was writing on behalf of her daughter. Apparently the mother had read one of my books and had concluded that the two of us—a forty-three-year-old writer and a twenty-year-old Bennington student—should become acquainted. I found the whole concept somewhat difficult to believe. The letter was the sort of unexpected plot development one might find in a nineteenth-century novel of manners. When I returned to Denver two weeks later, though, there it was. One afternoon I called the number. The father answered and observed that my timing was perfect. His daughter Anna had just returned that morning from New Zealand, where she had been climbing Mount Cook.

One thing led to another, as they sometimes do, and I found myself one week later picking up Anna at the Denver International

Airport. She saw me first and walked over with bright blue eyes and a broad smile. She had the muscular, lean body of an athlete and moved with the confidence and vigor of someone who has just ascended a snow-covered mountain in the Southern Hemisphere. Her hands were the strong weathered hands of a technical climber, and her hair was sandy-colored, with blond highlights from the alpine sun. Her nose and cheeks and the bottoms of her ears were still peeling. She spoke in rapid spurts and her voice was high and sharp. There was no subject about which she was not curious.

The next day we drove back out to the desert, she to join me in doing whatever it is I do out there in the desert. Not far from Arches National Park, there is a lovely road that leads from Seven Mile Canyon to Grandview Overlook. The asphalt road passes through a narrow box canyon where the rocks are scattered and broken, climbs a series of steep switchbacks, and then flattens out on a high plain where the grasses are thick. The wild pasture there—acres and acres, a windy bay extending in every direction—seems not part of the Red Rock Desert but a landscape imported from elsewhere, the plains of Mongolia or the savannas of East Africa. It is a place where one half expects to see a herd of Przewalski steppe horses or a reticulated giraffe. It was on that road, somewhere in the vicinity of Mesa Arch, that I expressed, as I sometimes do with travelling companions, my admiration for Weston's pioneering work in the California desert, and my intent to one day pursue my own vision along these lines. Anna, an avid photographer, was familiar with Weston and his milieu. To my surprise, for it certainly was not my intent, she declared that we should begin work on the project immediately.

The following day, in the Needles District of Canyonlands National Park, we did just that, and at a special place. Twenty years earlier I had gone out for a walk one morning and, over the

207

course of several hours, wandered a considerable distance off the trail. I had then gradually found myself inside a labyrinth of rocks that brought to mind the Greek parable of Theseus and Ariadne. It was an enclosed maze of passageways that simultaneously seemed to lead everywhere and nowhere. I eventually followed a deer path that led to a human trail that led to a four-wheel-drive track that led to a road that led me back to the world. Along the way, I discovered several things, not the least of which was a remarkable amphitheater I called "Point Solitude." The route to this sanctuary is about six miles in length, and winds through a network of red sandstone canyons. For the last two miles there is no trail, only a line-of-sight navigation over a series of slickrock ridges. Only a person who has been far off the traveled path in that part of the desert would ever find such a feature. Over the years I had often returned to the place, which had proven itself to be an ideal location for solitary camping and meditation.

When we reached Point Solitude our work began. To this day, some of those first photographs, taken with little regard for convention or concern for anything other than improvisation, are among my best. I will always be grateful to Anna for her courage, trust, and faith, as well as for her insight and imagination. In this process we were very much creative partners. Although I had by that time illustrated over a dozen books, photographing at locations ranging from the northern foothills of the Brooks Range to the depths of the Okefenokee Swamp, nothing in my experience had approached the challenge of fusing the human form to the desert landscape. It is one thing, in such a situation, to take a picture. It is quite another to create a work of art.

Over the next two weeks we sought to do just that. We found, among other things, that the time of day was even more important than is normally the case. Mid-day sun on desert rock is a harsh visual environment for the human form. The situation poses a number of challenges in terms of integrating the foreground with the landscape, as well as in striking a balance with the tonal scale. Although interesting effects can be achieved, as Weston and Charis often demonstrated in their collaborations, early morning and late afternoon offer a more forgiving light. We agreed that natural light was essential. We used no reflectors or flashes or shields. My subject was washed in whatever fell from the desert sky—unobstructed sunshine, diffuse cloudlight, the luminous glow that accompanies rain, the rich reflected light at the bottom of a sandstone canyon, the noonday shadow beneath a cottonwood tree, the brief fires of sunrise and sunset, the cold rays of a full moon setting on the Grand Canyon—and for this illumination we depended solely on god and the weather.

Our favorite place among these natural galleries, as we called them, was not a panoramic overlook, a picturesque ghost town, or a painted hoodoo garden. It was a nameless slot canyon in northern Arizona. These gulches are among the most unusual features in the Southwest—deep, narrow trenches in the desert floor formed by flash floods in the summer thunderstorm season. You pass through a portal, a gateway in the rock, and enter another world, a silent realm washed in warm red and orange light. In places the slot canyons are as narrow as your shoulders. Elsewhere they widen to accommodate your outstretched arms. Throughout, they are filled with soft reflected light, as the sunbeams are bounced off the smooth tapestried walls of golden sandstone. In the depths of these canyons there are otherworldly patterns of light and shade, hanging gardens on the walls, standing pools, desert owl nests, womblike silences, and striking petroglyphs scattered here and there. These places are magical, and I have often wondered what Weston and Charis could have done in such locations—in fact, I have often asked myself exactly what they would have done, because they had such fine artistic instincts.

When we returned from the desert, Anna decided to stay for the summer. We often hiked in the mountains with my son, who comes out during the warm months, and in August I introduced them both to one of my oldest friends, the Canadian Rockies. Along the way I taught her how to play the guitar and how to oil paint, and she soon exhibited her first works in a juried show. In the fall, though, she had to return to college and her promising future in the east. We had remained close friends throughout, but would now, because of the natural course of her life, see each other only rarely. I realized at that point that my work had only begun, and that the most essential part—the learning phase—was now complete. Her visit had been a blessing, one of those rare moments that life gives you, but the rest would now be up to me. In order to find a collaborator, I placed an advertisement in the local arts paper, explaining who I was and the nature of what was now a named book project *(One Hundred Photographs: The Female Form and the Desert Southwest)*. Over the course of the next week I received eighteen inquiries. Most were not suited for the project, a fact that became apparent as I explained that the task involved rising before dawn, hiking across endless dune fields, wading up seasonal rivers, following game trails when conventional paths gave way, trekking through slot canyons, climbing eroded rock pinnacles, and trying not to pass out while standing on the edge of a 900-foot cliff.

Six I agreed to meet with. All were in their early twenties. Their backgrounds could not have been more diverse—an artist, a photographer, a personal trainer, a physical therapist, a dancer, and a waitress. Ultimately I chose to work with a young woman named Christine. She had grown up in Muninsing, Michigan, the daughter of a ranger in the Hiawatha National Forest, and had spent whole weeks of her early life camping in the north woods with her father, mother, and sister. She would be comfortable in the desert. She bore a strong resemblance to Charis Wilson, and I could see the red hair would be beneficial, given the terra rosa hue of the prevalent Navajo sandstone. There was also a distinct echo, in her face and form, of Helga Testorf, the model with whom the watercolor and tempera painter Andrew Wyeth had worked so effectively in the 1970s.

There was finally this—Christine had experienced an unusually difficult life journey, and I believed the desert might be a healing landscape for her, as it had been so often for me. In the end she and I spent most of October in the desert, working clockwise from Arches National Park to Monument Valley to the north rim of the Grand Canyon, and then back north through Zion National Park, Bryce Canyon National Park, and Capitol Reef National Park. This was the same approximate route that Anna and I had taken in the spring. The advantage on the fall trip was that, in each location, I knew exactly where to go and, just as important, when to go during the day.

A year and a half passed. The project, which occupied an entire table in my office, was passed over as other pressing literary or photographic tasks came and went. The opportunity to work on the book arose again when my former New York editor, Laurel, traveled west for a spring visit. She was twenty-six and a graduate of Middlebury College. She worked as an English teacher at a private secondary school in Vermont and also served as the cross-country skiing coach. Both of her brothers were artists, and she had a broad knowledge of painting and photography. We had first met over the phone when she worked for one of my publishers in New York, and had developed a friendship, as people often do, through phone conversations and correspondence. During the course of our travels through the Red Rock Desert, Laurel expressed interest in the project, and so we worked at several locations, including Natural Bridges National Monument and Canyonlands National Park. I had begun to realize at this point that every human form presents its own unique landscape, and poses interesting challenges in terms of the basic objective of unifying foreground and background. Like Anna and Christine, Laurel was very much an equal partner in the task of composing images, and offered many compelling ideas in different situations.

What I learned over the course of these efforts was that, for all my years of exploring the desert, I knew little of it. I knew less of the human form and still less of the many obvious and subtle ways in which the two are bound together in a single harmony. Each time I anchored the tripod and held up the light meter, I was aware of my challenges and my responsibilities. I learned, too, that as the form is unclothed, so is the spirit, and that a muse may then share thoughts and memories which are normally withheld. Such epiphanies of pain or loss or hope are often absorbed into the compositional process, and are silently reflected in the image that will endure when those who made it have been returned to the earth. Throughout these trips, I made every effort to create images unlike any that have been seen before. I had no desire to imitate the past, or to record the visual moment as anything less than a revelation. Each image was a focused meditation, a celebration of the eternal present, and an attempt to honor all that is evoked by the word life.

III.

Twenty-two years ago, on a gray December day, I walked into a light-filled gallery of the Museum of Fine Arts in Boston and viewed the painting by Paul Gauguin (1848–1903) entitled *D'Ou Venons Nous? Que Sommes Nous? Ou Allons Nous?* Translated, these questions are "Where do we come from? What are we? Where are we going?" The over-sized painting stretches out to roughly five feet by twelve feet (54 inches by 147 inches). Gauguin worked on his masterpiece for a solid month in what he later described as an "unbelievably feverish state." There were no preparatory studies. He painted the scene wholly from his imagination. His canvas was a wrinkled piece of sac cloth. His brushes were whatever he could find in that remote place (the South Pacific). His paints were similarly improvised. Gauguin saw this complex image as his *ultimate verba,* his final statement to the world, a summary of all that he knew and wished he could know. Even then, in December 1897, he understood that his time among the living was limited.

The painting depicts a clearing in a forest. In the opening are twelve people—the old and young, sick and healthy, happy and sad. Some are clothed, others are unclothed. To the right of center a figure reaches for a ripe red fruit that carries with it all the symbolism of the Old Testament. Not far away, two young women sit pensively near a baby, its head turned in sleep. Elsewhere an elderly woman sits mournfully with her head in her hands. Nearby is a young woman, her eyes turned from the old woman. Behind them is a blue-green statue of a deity, the expression inscrutable. To the side a woman stands in profile, her eyes stealing a glance at the viewer. And there are others—a child eating a piece of fruit, two figures in nightclothes wandering down a path. In the far background one can see an ocean, a distant mountain, and drifting clouds. The color blue pervades the painting. Mixed into almost every other pigment, the dull ultramarine conveys an impression of melancholy. The painting can variously be looked at as an hallucination, a vision, or a penetrating examination. Perhaps even its creator did not know which.

In the upper left corner, against a golden background that is also the brightest region of the canvas, Gauguin boldly painted his three questions. I say "boldly" because at that time, before the more experimental era of Picasso and Braque, artists did not place philosophical questions on their paintings. It has often occurred to me, in this regard, that my desert figure studies are an attempt to visually respond to Gauguin's three questions—"Where do we come from? What are we? Where are we going?" Each person I photograph is a microcosm of the human race. Each scene I preserve is a concentrated fragment of the universe at large. Implicit in all of these images is, if not a series of answers, then an alternative framing of the questions. Taken as a whole, the suite is meant to remind us that we all come from nature and that we will all ultimately return to that realm, no matter where or how we live. The images are designed, in that sense, to be both uplifting and cautionary. Because of their setting, they also remind us of the oldest myth—that we, as a race, have wandered from the garden, but that, through the purity of art, which eschews all that is worldly, we can re-enter paradise, and be at one with it, again.

Notes on Contributors

Emma Brown is a graduate of Stanford University. She has traveled widely in western North America, including the Wind River Range, the northern Rockies in Idaho, the San Juan Islands of Washington, and Baja California. She currently resides in Juneau, Alaska. Her essays have appeared in journals and newspapers, including the *Washington Post*. This is her third appearance in the American Nature Writing series.

Leigh Calvez lives with her husband on an island near Seattle, Washington. She has worked around the world as a whale researcher, including the Azore Islands, New England, Australia, and Alaska. She is currently writing a book about Springer, the female killer whale that was orphaned by her family group, captured by scientists, and then returned to the wild waters near Vancouver Island, British Columbia.

Lauri Dane is an assistant professor of English at the State University of New York in Peru, New York. Her life experience includes advanced graduate training as a marine biologist and work as professional journalist. She has lived in Greece, Indonesia, Germany, and elsewhere. She is currently writing her first book, which is devoted to the human and natural landscape of Greece.

Jennifer DePrima lives in Manchester, New Hampshire, where she works in college administration and studies creative writing. Her essay speaks to the often unique relationships that women have with nature, especially nature in the wild context.

Penny Harter has in recent years published a number of poetry collections, including *Turtle Blessing, Lizard Light,* and *Buried in the Sky*. Her work appears widely in journals, and she has won fellowships and awards from the New Jersey State Council on the Arts, the Poetry Society of America, and the Geraldine R. Dodge Foundation. She lives with her husband in Summit, New Jersey. She was the first recipient of the William O. Douglas Nature Writing Award, selected by John A. Murray for *American Nature Writing 2002*. This is her fifth appearance in the American Nature Writing series.

April Heaney holds degrees in English from the University of Wyoming–Laramie, where she recently taught English for two years as an instructor. She is currently a doctoral student in English literature, with a creative writing (nonfiction) emphasis, at the University of Denver.

Dale Herring is a graduate of the University of Colorado, Boulder. She has worked for the Peace Corps in Honduras and has travelled widely in Latin America. She is currently the assistant director of the book division of the National Geographic Society. Her writings have appeared in American Whitewater and other publications. This is her second appearance in the American Nature Writing series.

Verna Johnston was a biology professor for thirty-seven years at San Joaquin Delta College. Her work has appeared in *Audubon, Sierra*, the *Christian Science Monitor,* and the *New York Times*. She is the author of several books, including *Sierra Nevada:*

The Naturalist's Companion and *California Forests and Woodlands: A Natural History,* both published by the University of California Press. She lives in Carmel Valley, California.

Kimberley A. Jurney is a sixth-grade special education teacher in the public schools of Bucks County, Pennsylvania, where she and her husband have lived for over ten years. Each summer she travels west to her second home, Yellowstone National Park, where she takes courses in nature writing and natural history at the Yellowstone Institute and spends as much time as she can wolf-watching.

Chinle Miller holds degrees in anthropology/archaeology and American Indian linguistics, and works as a freelance writer and editor in Moab, Utah. She is particularly interested in the relationship between language and nature. Her work has appeared in a number of nature books, including *Explore Capitol Reef National Park, 50 Best Wildflower Hikes in Utah, Red Twilight: The Last Free Days of the Ute Indians, Explore the Waterpocket Fold District,* and *Living in the Runaway West.*

Penelope Grenoble O'Malley is the recipient of three Los Angeles Press Club awards for journalism, writing on land use and environmental conservation. Her collection of essays on environmental ambivalence in Southern California's Santa Monica Mountains is forthcoming from the University of Nevada Press. This is her second appearance in the American Nature Writing series.

Adele Ne Jame is an assistant professor of creative writing at Hawaii Pacific University. She is the recipient of an NEA in poetry and served a year as poet-in-residence at the University of Wisconsin–Madison. Her work has appeared widely in journals, and she is the author of *Field Work,* a collection of poems. This is her fifth appearance in the American Nature Writing series.

Christine A. Petersen lives in Minnetonka, Minnesota, where she works as an elementary school teacher. Her students receive a special emphasis on environmental education, and she often organizes field expeditions to such locations as the Wolf Institute in Ely, Minnesota. Her writing is especially concerned with "how much wild nature is around us even in crowded urban and suburban areas."

Zorika Petic immigrated to the United States from the Balkans following World War II. She grew up in Ithaca, New York, spending much of her childhood on a dairy and horse farm. For many years she was a writer and editor at Cornell University. She lives with her husband in a rural area of Ithaca.

Gretel Schueller teaches writing at Plattsburgh State University in Peru, New York. Her writing has appeared in such magazines as *Audubon, Sierra, Discover,* and *Wildlife Journal.* She was for several years an editor at Audubon magazine.

Jill Robin Sisson is employed as an environmental educator at the Museum of the Hudson Highlands, where she develops and leads programs geared toward immersing children and their families in the outdoors. Her writings reflect her love for children and the outdoors, and her commitment to environmental education.

Gretchen Dawn Yost is a graduate in philosophy from the University of Oregon, Eugene. Her work has been widely published in journals and collections, including the American Nature Writing series. For the past six years she has lived in Pinedale, Wyoming, where she works as a backcountry ranger in the Wind River Range.

Permissions

Emma Brown: "Chamberlain." Copyright 2003 by Emma Brown.

Leigh Calvez: "A World Away." Copyright 2003 by Leigh Calvez.

Lauri Dane: "Where the Mountains Meet." Copyright 2003 by Lauri Dane.

Jennifer DePrima: "Fire Line." Copyright 2003 by Jennifer DePrima.

Penny Harter: "The Gravity of the Sacred," "Snow and Ash," "It Is Hard," and "Cartography," from *Buried in the Sky* (La Alameda Press). Copyright 2001 by Penny Harter. "Flies on the Corn," from *Gargoyle* #46. Copyright 2003 by Penny Harter. Reprinted by permission of the author.

April Heaney: "The Garden of Live Flowers." Copyright 2003 by April Heaney.

Dale Herring: "The Heron's Passport." Copyright 2003 by Dale Herring.

Verna Johnston: "Redwood Forest," from *California Forests and Woodlands: A Natural History* (University of California Press, 1994). Reprinted by permission of the author.